First Light

Nightfall Book Four

Jeffery Martin Botzenhart

Publisher's Note:

This is a work of fiction. All names, characters, places, and
events are the work of the author's imagination.

Any resemblance to real persons, places, or events is
coincidental.

Solstice Publishing - www.solsticepublishing.com

First Light

Nightfall – Book Four

By

Jeffery Martin Botzenhart

To you, my reader. My characters and I thank you for being a part of this journey.

Part One

The Still of the Night

Chapter One

Awakening amidst the still of the night, haunted once more by the same nightmare he suffered each time when closing his eyes, Ben Lesterman suddenly sat up in bed. With his body soaked in sweat, he covered his bare chest with his hand, his heart pounding beneath his skin. Recognizing it was only a bad dream, he rested his head back down on his pillow. Exhaling his fear, Ben stared up at his bedroom's dark ceiling, finding nothing scary there, knowing he wouldn't. In truth, the attic above was the space that frightened him most, the place where he found his father dead, as well as a damaged replicate, an exact duplicate of himself.

After dragging his father's body down the steps months ago, Ben had locked the attic door behind him, not intending to go up there again. Yet, from that moment on, he knew the answer to how his father died was still up there, if he could only find the courage to confront what happened. And just maybe, the answer to his mother's disappearance might be there too.

Rising from his bed, the wood floor creaked when walking over to the door. Swallowing hard, he stepped out into the darkened hallway, turning left toward the attic. Desperate in wanting to end his nightmares, he knew he couldn't go any longer without finding out the truth. Breathing hard, he reached for the lock that still had the key attached. Once the door was unlocked and open, he flipped on the light switch, while slowly climbing the steep steps up to the dimly lit attic, breathing in a musty smell when nearing the top step.

Drawing his eyes away from where he found his father's body, Ben looked at the replicate image of himself, sitting lifelessly in a chair near the window. Having learned all he could about synthetic replicates, from internet sites not monitored by the government, the answer to his question lay within the replicate's robotic head. Behind every replicate's right eye, a miniature spy camera was set, having the capacity to record for one year before requiring a replacement computer chip. All Ben had to do was detach this camera from the replicate and link it to a laptop, allowing for him to view every moment recorded.

Tilting the replicate's head back, using the moonlight flooding in through the dusty window to see with, when reaching into the gaping hole in its skull, Ben found the undamaged camera. Pulling it free from its holding mechanism, the camera fit easily in the palm of his hand. So absorbed in studying the camera, while stepping back, Ben was startled when the replicate fell out of the chair, its dead eyes staring at him. Unnerved by this, Ben quickly left, once more locking the attic door behind him while silently vowing never to go up there again.

Returning to his room, he powered up his laptop and linked the camera to a port at its side. Having downloaded a program to view the camera's recorded footage, he watched the screen as the first images appeared. His eyes nearly burst, stunned in witnessing the brutality his replicate waged against the citizens of Boston, men and women of all race and, disturbingly, children as well. It was no more than a mindless, killing machine. With the most terrible footage being revealed, his heart sank as he grew nauseated by the torture and death he saw.

Fast forwarding through the footage, the horror and carnage intensified until coming to a point when seeing an angry mob bashing the replicate with baseball bats and metal pipes. Ben nearly hyperventilated when his father's face appeared on screen. Seeing him struggle to get the replicate in the backseat of his car, left Ben wondering why he would do such a thing. Moving forward in the footage, the reason soon became apparent.

Staring at the screen, Ben's heart broke, watching how his mother acted as if the replicate were really him. Sitting with the replicate, reading to it, attempting to feed it and worst of all, kissing and embracing it, Ben saw how his mother grew more and more despondent. Breaking down, he wiped the tears from his eyes, regretting how devastated both his parents were.

The moment he dreaded most then shone on screen. While poking around within its head, his father must have done something to cause it to react violently. The following image showed his father's face, bloodied and almost lifeless. And then his father disappeared from sight.

Ben was just about to exit the program, not wanting to see anymore, when another face appeared on screen. Ben's breath rushed from his lungs, recognizing the last person seen through the replicate's camera.

***

Stepping outside, careful not to spill his coffee, Abdul walked over to where Scotty stood on the deck, joining his son in enjoying the tranquil summer morning. The warm sun was already high in the expansive, clear, blue sky reflecting its vivid color off the sound. Watching an eagle take flight, Abdul sipped his coffee, sighing contently after breathing in the aroma. Hearing the splashing of water, he turned his attention to Sebastian. Standing on shore, with Silas prancing at his feet, Sebastian cast a stick out into the water, for which Silas playfully rushed in after. Grabbing the stick with its teeth, dog-paddling back to shore, Silas returned with it, dropping the stick in Sebastian's palm. Then, shaking off the water vigorously, prancing once more, Silas seemed to beg for Sebastian to throw it again.

Seeing Scotty's sideways glance at him, Abdul patiently waited for his son to break the silence.

"He's so quiet. *Too* quiet. It's been seven months since Sebastian came home but a part of me isn't really sure that he *has* come home. I don't know," he said, exhaling his frustration. "Maybe it's nothing. Maybe I'm just imagining things that aren't there."

"No, you're not," Abdul responded. "In body, he's home. But I, too, can tell that his mind is far away from here."

"He's never said anything to me, in detail, about all that time away from us. I've tried asking him, but I know he's holding a lot back."

"Yes, there is much he's not telling us," Abdul commented, resting his hand on Scotty's shoulder. "I think we just need to give him some more time, keep making him feel safe until he is ready to reveal to us what he can't right now. I can only guess what he went through and, in truth, it would probably be much worse."

"Why won't he tell us? We could help him," Scotty argued.

"I believe he is the only one who can help himself," Abdul reasoned. "What you need to understand is that his heart and mind have repeatedly been plunged into darkness since he was very young. The emotional scars he carries are deeper than you could ever imagine. I believe he's doing his best to deal with them in trying to move on. It *will take time*. Pressing him for answers to questions he's not ready to face has the potential to damage him further. We're all in the midst of a silent storm with him. We simply must ride it out."

"That answer sucks."

"Yes, it does," Abdul responded thoughtfully while sipping more of his coffee.

***

Hearing a soft knock on his bedroom door, Scotty looked up from packing his suitcase. Exchanging a hesitant smile with Sebastian, Scotty watched him slowly enter, sitting on the edge of the bed.

"So, you're almost done packing for your big adventure to Los Angeles?"

"Yeah, Dad's looking forward to us seeing his mom and sisters before dropping me off at UCLA," Scotty responded.

"Are you nervous about being so far away from home?"

"To be honest, I'm more worried about feeling so exposed. Both Dads believe it will be safe being around all those people." Thinking for a moment, Scotty continued, "I don't know. I guess I'm just being paranoid."

"I understand. After San Francisco...well, I stayed away from the big cities," Sebastian revealed. "I liked the wide open spaces. It let me see what was coming. It just made me feel safer."

"Yeah," Scotty agreed, exhaling deep. "I'm just overthinking things like I usually do. I'll be fine. The only other thing I'll have to get used to is using a new last name. *Suarez*, what do you think?"

"How'd they pick *Suarez*?"

"It's my grandmother's maiden name."

"I should let you get back to packing." Appearing to struggle with something else to say, Sebastian stood up, turning toward the door. He stopped before walking out. "I'm sorry."

"For what?" Scotty urged, reaching out to him. "*Please*, tell me."

Sitting back down, Sebastian sighed deeply.

"After being gone for so long, I just wanted to find a place I could come home to. I can't thank your dads enough for offering to be my guardians. They're really great. But each night, when I go to sleep, I'm constantly dreaming about what happened in San Francisco and Maine and Canada. And, every day, I keep waiting for something bad to start. I know you want me to tell you about all those months away. Believe me, it's not that I'm trying to keep stuff from any of you, what I'm really doing is trying to keep stuff from myself. I don't want to remember any of it. I just want it all to go away."

"Did you ever wonder, I mean…did you ever wish that you didn't return to the dump and step in the daybreak chamber that first night we met?" Scotty asked, hesitating to bring up a thought that had bothered him for a long time.

"Would you hate me if I said yes?"

"No." Gripping Sebastian's trembling hands, Scotty smiled. "I think I understand now." Pulling him close, Scotty hugged Sebastian for the longest time, spying once over his shoulder and seeing Abdul's grinning nod when passing by his door. "You're gonna be okay," Scotty whispered.

"I don't believe you…but I hope so."

***

Having his shoulder rubbed by Abdul, with their foreheads pressed together, Sebastian noticed the concern in his expression.

"Are you sure you'll be okay alone? I wish you would come with us?"

No, I can't go back to California," Sebastian whispered, lowering his eyes.

"Los Angeles and Pasadena are far away from San Francisco."

"Not far enough away."

"I could stay home with you. Three weeks *is* a long time to be gone."

"No," Sebastian argued. "Scotty wants you both to help him get settled in at college. You need to be there with him. *Anyway*, I don't want to rob you of the chance to spend quality time with your mother-in-law in LA," he added, smiling.

"There is a mean streak in you. You know this?" Abdul whispered. He kissed his head. "Call me *anytime* if you need me. I love you."

"I love you, too."

Stepping back, he then turned to Scotty.

"UCLA's genius pool is about to double its intelligence." Hugging each other, Sebastian patted him on his back. "I'm gonna miss you."

"I'm gonna miss you, too," Scotty responded, smiling, though almost in tears.

"There are plenty of leftovers in the freezer when you get hungry," Xavier remarked, taking his turn in saying goodbye. "Make sure you do your laundry and keep the house clean."

"*Yes, Mom,*" Sebastian groaned, somewhat rolling his eyes before grinning. "I'll be fine."

"I know you will," Xavier said, himself becoming emotional when hugging him.

"You guys better get going if you want to reach Seattle tonight." Stepping back, Sebastian waved to them as they drove away. Then turning his attention to Silas, he ran his hands through the fur on his dogs head. "Let's get our stuff, boy. I want to get going as soon as we can."

Chapter Two

3 days later

Seagulls soaring through the sprawling, blue sky called out to each other over the hypnotic, rolling waves. Staring out at the crashing California surf, from the terrace of his mother-in-law's beach house, a comment from Xavier's mother, Marina, pulled Abdul away from his distracted thoughts.

"My son looks so very handsome with his hair cut short. Have you ever considered cutting your hair?"

"Not that I could recall. Your son prefers my hair long," Abdul replied casually to his mother-in-law. Glaring at him, Abdul smirked when Marina uncomfortably looked away. "Was it your second, or third husband, who had long hair? I can't seem to remember," he asked, watching her shift uneasily in her chair. The ringing of Abdul's cell phone drew his attention away from enjoying her discomfort.

"Always working," she commented, sounding noticeably irritated. "What *exactly* do you do? *Telemarketing*, perhaps?"

"I'm a technical consultant. *However*, I have been known to tell people where to go, and what to do when they get there. For family, these services are free."

"That must be why my son lives in a *guest house*," she mumbled, under her breath.

Paying little attention to her last comment, Abdul recognized the number of his incoming caller.

"My apologies," he offered, while standing up. "I need to take this in private." He continued, walking away from her.

"Mister Nassir, I have completed the diagnostic you requested on Dryden Technologies synthetic replicate program, now seized by the government," Maurice confirmed.

"And what were your findings?"

"Of the fifty-five thousand replicates generated and programmed, only four remain active, including me."

"Were you able to identify the other three?"

"Not entirely, sir. I was able to access only certain information pertaining to their unique design. Additional information such as facial profiles, identities, and current locations could not be accessed. Someone took great care to keep these three components secret."

"What other information on them is available? You mentioned unique design. How so?"

"All three are of an advanced generation of replicates, hybrids designated for one sole protocol."

"That being?"

"They were designed and programed to be assassins."

"So there is *no other* information on them than this?" Abdul asked, sighing while running his hand over his beard.

"There is one further aspect of their protocol available. Once their mission is complete, they will self-destruct. This poses a significant risk of human casualties were they to detonate in a public place. To be standing next to one would prove fatal."

"Did the program, in any way, reveal or suggest political target, either here or abroad?"

"Considering advanced replicate screenings at airports, with daily international flights, the certainty their targets are overseas is highly unlikely. I believe they were intended for domestic targets, possibly someone threatening the synthetic replicate program."

"The President, or the administration officials?"

"Both high profile and soft targets should be considered."

"What do you mean by *soft targets*?"

"Someone *appearing* as an unimportant average citizen. While seeming insignificant to you or me, *anyone* walking past either of us down the street could be holding information that the former administrators of the replicate initiative might view as damaging if revealed. A number of replicates committed what were viewed as senseless murders. Yet, if each case were thoroughly investigated, I believe a pattern would soon form, showing these individuals in a not so innocent light."

"A harmless secretary who may have mistakenly read classified information or a computer technician even remotely associated with software unknowingly meant for the replicates."

"Precisely, sir."

"Why hasn't the government tried remotely interfering with their protocols, rendering them harmless?" Abdul asked, taking a deep breath.

"Any tampering, or attempted corruption, of their programming will result in instant detonation. The President has yet to be convinced that the benefit of doing so outweighs the risk.

"But detonation *will* happen. Certainly, he must know this."

"Yes, sir. In analyzing data involving thirteen other replicates with assassination protocols, after killing their intended targets, all but one detonated with no additional loss of life. One replicate, however, just over a year ago, detonated in Time Square, killing thirty-five people. A government cover up deemed this an act of international terrorism, with innocent targets in The Sudan being bombed in retribution by the American military."

"So, they walk amongst us and we are powerless to stop them," Abdul commented, exhaling his frustration.

"Correct."

"Thank you for this update, my friend. Please keep me posted on any further developments."

"Unfortunately, that will not be possible, sir. My own termination is rapidly advancing."

"How so?" Abdul uttered, overwhelmed with concern.

"All my efforts evading government agents have unfortunately met their end. I am currently sitting on a park bench, in the Mission District, here in San Francisco. As we speak, government agents are converging on my position. Their weapons are drawn and they have been instructed with termination orders for me."

"I'm sorry, my friend. I wish there was something I could do to help," Abdul offered, closing his eyes.

"So this call may not be traced, I am concluding our conversation and destroying this cell phone. It has been a pleasure serving you, sir. Have a wonderful day." With the call abruptly ending, Abdul glanced down at his phone screen, now blank.

Forcing aside his regrets for Maurice, Abdul's grave concern over the remaining three replicates and their assassin protocols prompted him to make an urgent call.

***

The day had started out bright and sunny but, by early afternoon, dark clouds threatening storms appeared on the horizon. From what Sebastian heard on the radio, the entire state of Nebraska was under a severe weather warning with the probability of tornadoes touching down any time after noon. A funnel cloud had already been spotted on the Nebraska-Wyoming border.

Although he'd been to his uncle's farm before, having been detoured due to road construction, Sebastian found himself lost among vast fields of corn seen in every direction. Stopping at a lonely intersection, he and Silas got out stretching their legs. With the GPS on his cell phone hopelessly confused, Sebastian leaned back against the jeep, feeling lightheaded from the extreme, July heat. Glancing down at the tremors shaking his hands, he exhaled his exhaustion, wanting nothing more than a cold drink and a nap.

Watching the clouds on the western horizon growing darker and darker, Sebastian was nearly blown off his feet by a strong gust of heated wind. Feeling Silas nudging his leg, he looked down, seeing how anxious his dog was acting.

"I know boy, we're in for one heck of a storm." The sound of rolling thunder confirmed this.

Hearing his cell phone, Sebastian pulled it from his pocket, recognizing his caller.

"Hey, what's up?"

"How are you?" Abdul asked, sounding tense.

"Oh, you know, I guess I'm feeling a little—lost," Sebastian answered in truth. The booming sound of thunder seemed to shake the jeep and the ground under his feet.

"What? Is that the sound of a storm I hear? I checked the weather report for Alaska this morning. You're supposed to have sun all day."

With his eyes growing large, just north of him Sebastian spied a funnel cloud threatening to drop a tornado.

"Oh, I'm just watching some old movie on television," Sebastian lied, thinking fast.

"What movie?"

"*Twister.*"

"You're right. That's an old movie."

"The special effects are amazing. Hey, listen. I'm really tired. I haven't been sleeping well."

"Go, turn off the television and take a nap," Abdul ordered. "I'll talk to you later."

"*Wait*! Why'd you call?"

"It's nothing. I was just worried about you." Something in the tone of his voice, leading Sebastian to believe there was more to this call, caused him concern. It wasn't like Abdul to keep things hidden.

"I'll be okay."

"I'll call you later."

"How 'bout I call *you* later, after I wake up?" Sebastian suggested, unsure of where he'd be.

"Yeah, that sounds better." After a short pause, Abdul added, "I love you."

"I love you, too. I'll talk to you later." Hanging up, Sebastian petted Silas on the head. "Come on, boy. We're gonna turn around and try to outrun the storm."

***

An hour later, with the sky clearing, Sebastian pulled the jeep into a small, run-down gas station in the middle of nowhere. Getting out, he watched as Silas found a place to do his business before stepping inside. Finding a vintage soda machine, he dropped some quarters in for a glass bottle of cherry cola. He heard someone walk up behind and turned around to see who it was.

"Well, aren't you just the cool drink of water I've been dying for all day," a grey-haired, older woman wearing a halter top and blue jeans flirted, with her smoky voice while approaching the cash register. Running her fingers down from his bare shoulder to his elbow, she asked, "What can I get you, baby?"

Amused by her not-even-remotely-subtle attention, Sebastian smiled.

"Now, I bet you call all the boys baby," he commented, playfully.

"No, only the handsome ones like you," she answered, cackling, motioning to his soda. "I'll give you another for the road—if I get to see what's under that cut off t-shirt of yours?"

"Gosh, you are one dirty old woman, aren't you?"

"Looking into those gorgeous eyes of yours, well, it's hard for woman like me to control myself," she teased, grinning. "Anyway, sugar, what's your pleasure?"

"Could you give me directions to Chancellorsville? I'm pretty lost."

"*Pretty*, oh *yes*, but not really that lost, baby," she answered, pointing to the left. "Down the road, about a mile, you'll come to an intersection. Turn right and Chancellorsville will be two miles ahead. But, your uncle's house will only be one mile in that direction."

"*What*?" Not believing what she said, Sebastian stood there, growing anxious while staring at her.

"Relax, baby, I've been friends with the Dryden's for years."

"How do you know I'm related to them?"

"Because you look so much like Lee. If I was to guess, I'd bet he was your dad," she answered, appearing thoughtful.

Feeling even more uncomfortable, he turned to leave but stopped for a moment when she said, "I'm so sorry for your loss. No one saw that coming. Honey, my name is Susan." Stepping in front of him, she offered, "If you need *anything*—no matter what it is, you just come back and ask." Giving him a peck on the cheek, she stepped out of his way.

"Thanks," he mumbled, looking down, and walking away. When outside, he called for Silas. Padding over to him, Silas licked his hand before jumping up into the Jeep. When driving away, he glanced out his window, seeing Susan watching him leave.

Chapter Three

Driving up to his uncle's farm, Sebastian parked on a dirt driveway next to the barn. Getting out, he noticed Silas sniffing around as if trailing the scent of something and was then surprised when Silas climbed the porch steps and laid down under a hanging swing, acting as if he'd lived here his whole life. Looking around, the farm seemed just as he remembered it from the last time being here. But the sky was different, watching more storm clouds drawing closer from the west and hearing the barn's weather vane turning. The white sheets hanging from a clothesline fluttered like ghosts, or sails, in the strong, warm breeze.

The mild banging of the barn door drew Sebastian's attention in that direction. Wandering over, he looked through the window seeing an old, red tractor parked inside. Tempted to wanting to sit on it, Sebastian entered through the partially open door. Passing a shaft of light beaming down from an upper window, he approached the tractor slowly, roaming his fingers over the dirty treads of a large, back tire while noticing rust spots here and there. Climbing up, he sat on the dusty, black seat with his hands running from the top of the steering wheel to the bottom.

Glancing to his left, the farm tools hanging on the wall were exactly what he expected to see. But when looking to his right, he spied something covered by a large, brown tarp. Intending to climb down to peek under it, Sebastian changed his mind when hearing a car door close outside. Jumping off, he walked over to the nearest window and saw a white pickup truck parked next to the house.

He heard a woman's voice talking to Silas as he stepped outside the barn.

"Come here, I won't hurt you," her voice called out, soothingly, to his dog. Wagging his tail, Silas scampered over to her, panting while obviously enjoying the attention. "Are you lost? I wonder where you came from."

Passing by the first line of hanging sheets, Sebastian caught glimpse of the woman, instantly recognizing her from a picture shown to him by his dad. While watching her, Sebastian's mind reeled in wondering how she was alive, after being told she'd died in the same car accident when he was abducted years ago. Though, knowing she wasn't his biological mother, she was the one who'd given birth to him. And, thinking back, he now realized his uncle hadn't lied to him when trying to get him to come inside last time he was here. His mom really was inside.

Wondering if she'd even recognize him in any way, Sebastian didn't know how to introduce himself to her. *And what if she wouldn't believe him if he told her he was her son?* Finally deciding to judge her reaction when seeing him, he exhaled deep before stepping into her sight.

"He's my dog," Sebastian said, causing her to turn around. Her stunned expression greeted him as she appeared at a loss for words. "My name's Sebastian."

Swallowing hard, she uttered, "Hello," while continuing to stare at him. "I'm your—I mean, I'm— Melinda," she struggled to introduce herself.

"Is my uncle here? I was hoping I could talk to him," Sebastian asked, uncomfortable under her watchful eyes.

Watching a tear stream down her cheek, when brushing strands of her wind-blown, brown hair away from her face, she answered, "He's...here. Come on. Follow me." Leading him toward the backyard, they walked just beyond the silo until stopping near a large tree at the edge of the field.

"Kurt, your uncle, died almost a month ago," she choked out, sniffling while brushing more tears away.

"How?" Sebastian asked, not taking his eyes off his low gravestone.

"He was coming home from town one night. His truck went off the road—and he died when it flipped over," Melinda answered, glancing blankly out at the field while nervously running one hand over the other.

"I'm sorry," Sebastian offered, quietly. "Does my dad know?" He clearly caught her off-guard.

"I didn't have the heart to tell him," Melinda mumbled, weakly, covering her mouth.

Before Sebastian could say anything else, everything in sight began spinning, causing him to stagger and fall to one knee.

"Are you alright?" He heard the panic in her voice.

"I'm a little dizzy. I'm not really feeling well," he answered, closing his eyes taking several deep breaths.

"Put your arm around me," Melinda urged. "I'll help you inside."

Draping his arm behind her neck, his light-headedness grew worse when standing. Through blurred and hazy vision, Sebastian felt more disoriented with each step and was barely able to climb the porch steps. Once inside the house, she led him to the sofa, insisting he lay back.

"I'll get you some water," she said, rushing away from him.

With Silas nudging his tremoring hand, Sebastian reached down, petting his dog.

"I'll be okay, boy. I'm just a little tired." Everything then faded to black.

***

Stirring when hearing a sound near him, Sebastian shifted his head to the side, opening his eyes.

"Welcome back. You gave me quite a scare," Melinda whispered, forcing a smile while sitting next to him on the edge of the sofa. Reaching over, she massaged his trembling hand.

"How long was I out?" he mumbled, groggily.

"You slept for about five hours. Are you hungry?"

"A little."

"What do you like?"

"Anything's fine."

"I'll be back in a few minutes. Don't go passing out on me again," Melinda said, with a more relaxed smile.

Feeling movement over his feet, Sebastian glanced over, seeing Silas resting on the blanket covering his legs. His ears perked up as Sebastian stretched his fingers out to pet him.

"Hey, boy. Thanks for keeping me company."

"Except for a few minutes, he hasn't left your side," Melinda revealed, returning with a peanut butter sandwich and a glass of milk.

"Thanks," Sebastian said, sitting up as he took the plate from her. While taking a bite, he watched as she nervously walked over to the front window, looking out into the darkness. Hearing the rumble of thunder, he guessed a storm was coming. He also guessed that she might be struggling to find something to say to him. When sitting down in an easy chair across the room from him, her expression was that of someone desperate to tell a secret, but sworn not to.

Wanting to break the silence, Melinda fell apart when Sebastian said, "I don't blame you for any of what happened to me,"

"But you should. It's—all my fault," Melinda choked out, softly, holding her hands to her chest as if stricken by terrible pain in her heart.

"Mom," Sebastian argued, calmly, seeing her skin turn pale. "It's not your fault. I survived. I'll be okay." Slowly rising from the sofa, he unsteadily walked over to her, extending his hand for hers. And, when standing in front of him, she hugged him tightly for the first time since he was four years old.

"Don't cry anymore. I don't blame you. Please," Sebastian whispered in her ear, stroking her hair.

"I've waited so long for this," Melinda blurted out.

"Me, too."

***

Sitting next to his mom, lazily moving on the porch swing, Sebastian watched the sporadic burst of light from fireflies out in the darkness of the front yard. Surprising to him, the air outside felt much warmer than before, as if the set sun continued heating the still of the night. Running his toes through Silas's soft fur, his dog seemed sound asleep at his feet. His mom looked tired too, but he thought she was keeping herself awake, wanting their time together to last. She finally broke their silence.

"So, what made you decide to come back here? I wasn't sure you ever would."

"For months I've been thinking about coming here, but convinced myself not to. I guess I just needed some time to work things through in my head. I can't move on a build a life for myself until I deal with what happened in the past."

"I understand."

"It was, like, putting a puzzle together until I ran out of pieces. That's why I decided to come here. I wanted to talk to Uncle Kurt about Dad. I know he's alive, somewhere. Hopefully Lydia is, too."

"Oh, honey, there's so much you don't know," she whispered, taking hold of his hand.

"I guess I just want to understand why he left me behind. Do you know where he is? Do you think you could talk to him for me—and find out why he and Lydia left like they did? I need to know."

"I think the best you could do is talk to him yourself. You don't have to go far, just over to the barn."

"You mean he's *here*?" Sebastian uttered, completely shocked.

"In a manner of speaking, *yes*." His mom said, standing up. "Come on. I'll take you as far as I can to him."

"Stay, boy," Sebastian told Silas. He followed his mom off the porch and over to the barn. Turning on an overhead light, Melinda walked over to the tarp Sebastian had seen earlier. Tugging on it, the tarp fell down, revealing a Daybreak chamber underneath.

"How many of these did Dad make?" Sebastian wondered, while watching her plug the chamber's cord into an electrical outlet.

"There are only two left now, this one and another one in Boston with Sidney."

"When did Sidney leave Montreal?"

"A few months ago."

"So Dad's been with Sidney the whole time?"

"Yes. Honey, I'm sure he'll explain everything to you, just—let him talk before you punch him this time."

"Oh, you know about that." Sebastian felt embarrassed by this.

"He deserved it."

"That's what Uncle Kurt said."

"Climb in. I think you know how this works. You'll see him in a minute."

"Do you…want me to tell him about Uncle Kurt?"

"Yes, if you would? I think it might be better coming from you," she responded, partly smiling while stepping away. "I'll be waiting on the porch."

After watching her leave, Sebastian climbed in the chamber. Placing the headphones on, he then pressed a button on the keypad and waited. Hearing a humming sound, a light blinded him momentarily, with his eyes adjusting when seeing a brilliant yellow sun setting in a fiery-orange, afternoon sky.

Chapter Four

Stepping out through the open barn doors, Sebastian squinted from the sunset's brilliant light shining in his eyes. Glancing to his right, he saw his dad standing at the edge of the back field, appearing lost to his thoughts. Crossing the yard quietly, approaching his dad, Sebastian felt his heart in is throat, not really knowing what to say to him. He stopped when his dad heard him and turned.

"Hey, Dad," Sebastian greeted, softly.

"Hey, kiddo."

"I—I'm—I'm sorry." Swallowing deep, Sebastian uncomfortably shifted his weight from one side to another.

"You don't have anything to be sorry about. Damn, I made a mess of things," Lee uttered, crossing the distance to his son.

"I don't know what to say," Sebastian mumbled anxiously, his pulse and breathing growing rapid.

"I do," Lee said, stepping in front of him. Feeling his dad tenderly run his hand through the hair on the side of his head, Sebastian exhaled his nerves and then fell apart when his dad hugged him.

"I love you, kiddo." After several minutes of silence, Lee took a step back, rubbing his hand across Sebastian's tear-soaked cheek staring into his son's eyes. "There's something I need you to do for me."

"What?"

Recognizing the tension is his dad's half-smile, Sebastian's heart sank as his father spoke.

"I *need* you to leave Nebraska as soon as you can."

"*Why?*" Sebastian forced out, breathlessly.

"Kiddo, it's not safe for you there. To be honest, I'm not sure *where* it would be safe for you."

"I don't understand."

"Listen to me. What happened in Alaska was no accident. There were people after me. I'd spent months trying to keep you, your sister, and me hidden from them. But, in the end, there was no hiding. They found me before I could get the three of us away from there."

"Who are they?"

"Government agents acting on orders from the President. I was on the brink of exposing one of the military's highest generals for her involvement with covert replicate operations when the President panicked, fearing he'd be implicated as well. What I didn't fully understand, until too late, was how far up in the government the ties to the replicate crisis reached."

"So, they came after you."

"They're coming for *anyone* even remotely connected to the replicate program. The scientists, programmers, technicians, executives, and even their families. Guilt by association. They want to wipe the slate clean, covering their tracks at all costs and making it look like nothing ever happened."

"So how did you end up with Sidney?"

"The day before the accident I called her, asking her to fly to Anchorage as soon as she could. I wanted her to take both you and Lydia back to Montreal with her and then disappear until I felt sure it was safe again."

"So you're both with Sidney right now?"

Lee nodded his head.

"Your uncle and Sidney worked together to make that happen. I'm guessing we're still together."

"What do you mean?"

"Lydia *was* here with me—but she isn't anymore," his dad revealed, covering his mouth with his hand.

"Where is she?"

"I'm not sure." Resting his hand on Sebastian's shoulder, Lee continued, "Kiddo, I know this is going to come as a shock to you and…I don't know how to make this sound okay. Through what your Uncle Kurt has heard from Sidney, I found out that both your sister and I suffered traumatic injuries when my SUV was run off the road. I was told that Lydia had sustained a severe head injury, and would probably never wake up. As for me, somewhere I'm currently on life support. My heart and lungs were damaged beyond repair. Clinically, I guess I'm dead except for my mind. To keep us alive, your uncle and Sidney found a way to give both your sister and I access to a Daybreak chamber. Kurt and I had talked about something like this a long time ago, for patients who suffered brain injuries and total body paralysis. I guess our theory works."

"I don't understand. Why can't Sidney find a way to heal your body? There has to be something that can be done?"

"There isn't kiddo. My injuries from the accident were too severe to recover from."

Sebastian thought this through.

"Well, at least you're still alive. You said before that people could stay in the Daybreak for a long time."

"But...not forever," Lee reminded him.

"So where's Lydia? Do you think she died?" Sebastian asked, reeling from confusion and sadness. "Is that why she can't access the program anymore?" His heart broke just asking this question.

"Maybe Sidney was wrong and she woke up," Lee answered, sounding hopeful, running his hand over his beard.

With his chin quivering, trying to process what his dad revealed, feeling overwhelmed. Sebastian took a step back. Blankly staring out, he felt his dad pulling his face back to him.

"I'm so sorry, kiddo." Sebastian could barely focus, unable to respond.

"Sebastian, listen to me. Look at me. Kiddo, you have to leave Nebraska."

"What, what about, Mom?"

"I'm glad you found her. But you have to listen to me. You're going to have to convince her and Uncle Kurt to leave with you. Kurt understands how dangerous things will get. You'll be safe with him."

"He can't help us," Sebastian blurted out. "Uncle Kurt died in a car accident a month ago." Realizing what he said, he added, "I'm sorry, Dad."

Seeming lost in thoughts, his dad sighed deeply.

"Maybe it wasn't an accident. What did your mom tell you about him?" His expression appearing grave.

"She said he was coming home from town one night when his truck went off the road. He died when it flipped over."

"Kurt wouldn't have had any reason to drive into Chancellorsville after dark. It's a strange little town. Everything closes by seven," his dad commented, looking frustrated with closed eyes.

"Mom didn't say which town he was driving from. Maybe he was coming home from somewhere else," Sebastian reasoned.

"No," his dad rejected this. "I'm not trying to scare you, kiddo but Kurt hated going out after dark. I can't imagine what would've made him go driving at night. There's something wrong about this." He ran his hand through Sebastian's hair once again. "This is why you need to get out of Nebraska—*now*."

"Where should Mom and I go?" Sebastian asked, worried and growing panicked. "We could go back to our house in Alaska?"

"No, you can't go back there," Lee insisted. "And you'll also have to warn Scotty and his dads to leave as soon as they can."

"They aren't there. Scotty and his dads are in California, dropping him off at college."

"You'll have to tell them they can't go back."

"I will."

"Go to Boston. Find Sidney and, hopefully, your sister. Your mom should have her phone number or address. Then...."

Sebastian's eyes nearly exploded from their sockets when his dad's image distort before pixelating. His dad then instantly disappeared from sight, leaving Sebastian shuddering in fear. For a minute he stood there alone, his eyes drawn to the creeping darkness as the crest of the setting sun vanished on the horizon.

***

Seeing his mom still sitting on the porch swing, Sebastian rushed up to her.

"Mom, we need to leave now! Dad said it's not safe here."

Reaching for his hand, she attempted to calm him.

"It's alright, honey. Sit down, *please*," she urged him. Confused by the ease in her expression, Sebastian hesitantly sat next to her. "Listen to me. This farm is *safe*. No one is going to hurt you here."

"But...Dad said—."

She cut him off.

"That we're in danger here," she continued. "It just *isn't* true. Sebastian, listen to me. When Kurt went to see your dad last, he noticed how paranoid and disturbed he'd become, fearful of some conspiracy against him and you and your sister. Kurt later questioned Sidney about this. Reluctantly, Sidney told him she'd injected your dad with an experimental drug, something to enhance brainwave activity, with one of the side effects being aggressive paranoia.

Some parts of what your dad claimed *were* true. Both he and Lydia were in an accident. Sidney did, in fact, fly to Alaska. But she was growing concerned about your dad's irrational, mental state. And, after the accident, with

Kurt's help, Sidney began direct care for your dad and Lydia at a private hospital just outside Montreal."

"But, everything he said—."

Melinda interrupted him again.

"Made sense to you because of all you've been through," she commented. "It all seemed so real because, to *him*, it all *is* real. His overstimulated brainwaves have dangerously heightened his anxiety levels to the point where he can't even process rational thoughts."

"Why did you want me to see him if you knew all this?" Sebastian asked, standing up, taking a step away without looking at her.

"I wasn't trying to be cruel. I promise. It's that I wasn't sure you'd believe me if I just told you all this without proof. I thought you should see it for yourself and, then, I could help you sort everything out." Rising from her seat, she walked over to him, wrapping her arm around his waist while leaning her head against his shoulder. "I'm sorry for putting you through all that. Please forgive me.

"Say something," she begged, quietly after a long pause.

"I—I'm—just tired."

"Come on. It's time for bed."

Something's not adding up, Sebastian thought to himself. *Dad acted the same way he always did with me. What am I missing?*

"Mom, could you call Sidney for me?" Sebastian asked, remaining still but driven by his growing suspicions.

"Why?"

"I'm running low on my medicine. Maybe she could have some sent here."

"What kind of medicine?"

"It's a special pill I take for my Parkinson's disease."

"I'll send her a text message," she said, pulling her cell phone out of her pocket.

"She won't answer a text, something she said about hating technology."

"Alright, I'll call her. It's close to midnight there but I'm sure she's still awake."

"Could I talk to her?"

"Of course." He thought he sensed some tension in her voice but wasn't certain. After dialing the number, Melinda handed him her cell phone. Looking down at the screen, Sebastian read the phone number to himself, instantly remembering each digit.

"Hi, you've reached Sidney. I'm probably off doing something fabulous, so I can't answer right now. Please leave your name and phone number and I'll get back to you as soon as I'm sober."

Hearing the beep after her message, rather than leaving a message, Sebastian hung up.

"We can try calling Sidney in the morning," he said, handing the phone back to her.

***

Feeling his cell phone buzzing in his pocket, Abdul pulled it out to see who was calling this late. But, when glancing at the screen, his eyes grew large while watching live video footage from their house in Alaska. Months ago, he'd installed a sophisticated, home security system linked to a special phone app. Should anyone breaking in trip the silent alarm, a live video feed would be sent to his cell phone along with police notification of a burglary.

Spying at least half a dozen men ransacking room after room, Abdul instantly worried for Sebastian's safety. Yet, in watching, he felt relieved that neither Sebastian nor Silas were there in the house. But seeing this caused him to wonder where they were. Fearing they might be hiding from the men, or possibly having been caught outside the house, Abdul watched helplessly, knowing he couldn't call Sebastian's cell phone for fear of leading the men in finding him and also potentially exposing their current location in California.

Startled in seeing a man's face appear on his screen, Abdul guessed that his hidden camera had been found. Ending the call before it could be traced, he used a special, cell phone scatter signal Scotty had designed to hide their location.

Seeing Xavier walking up to him, Abdul tossed his phone aside while attempting to hide his fear.

"It's late. I'm going to bed," Xavier said, kissing Abdul. "Are you alright?"

"Yes, I'm just tired," Abdul lied. "I'm coming to bed soon. I just want to watch a few minutes of the news." Faking a quick smile, his answer seemed to convince Xavier. Left alone, he turned on the television, staring at the screen blankly with his mind fighting to control the fear he felt for Sebastian's safety.

Chapter Five

With his eyes fixed on a sliver of light, under his closed bedroom door, Sebastian noticed a shadow move past before hearing his doorknob being turned. Closing his eyes, he breathed deeply in and out, pretending to be asleep while hearing the door open and then footsteps nearing his bed. Feeling Silas awaken, moving at the foot of the bed, he then heard his mom try quieting his dog when coming closer. After softly kissing him on the cheek, creaks in the floorboards revealed her stepping away. Spying out through one eye, Sebastian then watched his mom search through his backpack, clearly frustrated in not finding something. Knowing what she might be looking for, before climbing in bed, he'd turned off his cell phone hiding it under his nightstand.

Hearing his mom close the door behind her, Sebastian sat up, petting Silas before rising from the bed. Placing his ear against the bedroom door's wooden surface, he listened for a moment. Thinking she might have gone downstairs, Sebastian was surprised when hearing her voice.

"It's me. I'll be there in about fifteen to twenty minutes. Of course, I'm coming alone."

Hearing her go downstairs, Sebastian rushed in pulling on his jeans and sneakers.

"Stay, boy," he whispered to Silas. As quiet as possible, he opened his door and stepped out into the dark hallway. Seeing soft light from the bottom of the stairs, he waited until everything went dark before slowly making his way down to the living room. The ticking of a wall-mounted clock, and the humming from the kitchen refrigerator, were the only sounds heard as he tip-toed over to the front door. Peeking out through the curtain, he watched his mom walking away, down the dirt road leading in the opposite direction of Chancellorsville.

Barely able to see through the outside darkness of the moonless night, Sebastian left the house, nearly tripping over a garbage can when following his mom at a distance and also looking up occasionally in viewing the expansive stars overhead. Keeping to the road's grassy edge allowed him to conceal his footsteps while listening to her shoes grinding on the stone and dirt surface.

Following her, he wondered where she could be heading this late at night, as well as who she spoke to. Knowing town lay a mile in the other direction, the only place he recalled being close by was the old gas station where he'd asked for directions. Until reaching the farm, he remembered seeing no other houses near. Being that she'd called someone, maybe he'd see headlights when they'd reach the intersection, someone waiting there to talk to her. Clearly, by not driving, his mom didn't want to alert him that she'd left the house, possibly realizing the noise her truck would have made when backing out the driveway.

When approaching the intersection, Sebastian saw his mom's silhouette and shadow from the dim light shone from far above on a pole. So faint was the light, that even when reaching the stop sign, the word *STOP* could hardly be read. Having watched her walk left, he wondered if, in fact, she was heading for the old gas station.

Soon enough, the lit gas station sign, flashing as if ready to burn out, corrupted the darkness just up the road. Stepping over to one of the pumps, his mom stopped walking, anxiously glancing in all directions as if waiting to be frightened by something hiding in the dark. Warm, stray breezes passing though the cornstalks surrounding the gas station sullied the still of the night, seeming to add to her jumpiness. Staying hidden in the shadows of these cornstalks, Sebastian kept his eyes focused on his mom until hearing the office door of the gas station open.

Walking slowly up to her, Susan, the old woman who'd given him directions, stopped near his mom.

"So, what have you found out?" Susan asked, coughing sickly after lighting a cigarette.

"Nothing yet," Melinda answered, nervously pacing.

"You remember our deal?"

"Of course I do!" his mom answered, abruptly, the panic in her tone clear. "I just need some more time."

"How much more?" Susan asked, taking another drag from her cigarette.

"I don't know. My son doesn't have a cell phone. And, he hasn't said anything about them."

"Then make him. He has to know where they've gone. Both houses in Alaska have been searched. No computers, cell phones, or mobile devices were found. I can't stress enough to you the importance of finding the Nassir family. If you fail, the deal is off."

"How can you say that?" Melinda yelled.

"*Keep your voice down*," Susan growled.

"We're miles from anyone. Who's going to hear us?" Melinda argued, loudly, pointing her finger at the old woman. "I gave up the man I loved so my son could be safe. Kurt didn't know anything about those damned robots."

"Replicates," Susan corrected her.

"Who the hell cares what they're called! As far as I'm concerned they're killers...and my husband didn't know anything about them."

"We couldn't take any chances that he did," Susan argued back.

"*You bitch*," Melinda choked out when bursting to tears. "You forced me to choose between my husband and son."

"A choice you willingly made," Susan responded. "Believe me, we've all had to make sacrifices."

"I'm sure you didn't have to choose between two people you love—for one of them to die."

"I've made more sacrifices and hard choices than you'll ever know," Susan revealed, coldly, blowing smoke from her mouth and flicking her cigarette down on the ground. Years ago, when I joined Special Ops, I made a solemn vow to serve and protect my country at all costs. And, in doing so, I was forced to sacrifice my humanity. I was forced to come to terms with that a long time ago. I suffocated and buried my beloved husband when finding out he was spying for the Russians. And, I helped send my own son to a military prison in Kansas for dereliction of duty, running away from a battle in Iran because he was too scared to fight. The first time I went to visit him he told me to never come back. Believe me, I haven't. As for your husband, I've known Kurt since he was a baby. It wasn't easy for me to run him off the road that night, or watch him beg for help until he died. But I did what I had to do, just as you will. Now, either come back tomorrow night with an answer, or find one incredible out-of-reach, hiding place for you and your son."

"You're a monster," Melinda uttered.

"One worse than you could imagine—when need be."

***

Once far enough away from the gas station, Sebastian ran through the cornfields, stopping a few times when disoriented by which direction to go. Stumbling several times over ruts in the ground, he eventually saw the dim intersection light. Then sprinting on the roads edge, about ten minutes later he found the house.

With his chest heaving to catch his breath and barely able to climb onto the porch, when stepping inside, he headed up the staircase to his bedroom. Feeling his body soaked with sweat, he knew he didn't have enough time to shower or towel off before his mom returned. Tugging off his jeans and kicking off his shoes, Sebastian froze when hearing the front door open. And, just after crawling under the sheet, he heard his doorknob being turned.

Still trying to catch his breath, thinking fast, he closed his eyes and pretended suffering through a nightmare. Breathing fast and shifting uncomfortably under his sheet, his deception must have been convincing. Sensing her weight on the edge of his bed, when touching his damp hair he heard his mom fret.

"Oh, honey, it will be alright. It's just a bad dream, nothing more." She stayed by his side until he gained control of his breathing and was able to fake falling asleep.

Lying still after his mom left his side, Sebastian stared out, his mind overwhelmed by what he heard. Everything his dad said to him was true, with everything his mom saying, a lie. And hearing that she'd sacrificed her husband for him left Sebastian astounded that anyone could make such a choice. *How does one look at two people they love and decide which one lives and which one dies? How could she just stand by and not fight for both of them? And if given another choice between her and him, would his mom choose to save herself?*

Even more disturbing to Sebastian was how willing his mom would be to turn over Scotty and his dads for them to be killed. They weren't just strangers, they were his family too. There was no way he would let her help the government hurt them. So, for the next few hours, plan-after-plan played out in his mind, with escape being the first.

***

Hearing the shower running, Melinda rolled over in bed, rubbing her eye, feeling exhausted from tossing and turning all night. Glancing out her bedroom window, seeing the day's first light on the low edge of the eastern horizon, for a moment she smiled.

"An early riser, just like his dad," she mumbled.

Closing her eyes for a minute, she wanted to cry when thinking back to last night's meeting with Susan at the gas station. While desperately trying to figure out how to get Sebastian to tell her about the Nassir family, her thoughts couldn't let go of finding Sebastian gripped by his nightmare. *How many nights had he suffered alone like that? And with all he'd gone through, how could she ever find a way to end this agony for him when she hadn't even found a way to end her own?* The pain and shame of what she'd done to Kurt would never leave her.

The worst thought of all then crept in her mind. *What if she failed?* Although believing Sebastian would tell her enough about where the Nassir family currently was neither her, nor Sebastian, would be safe until the Nassir's were found and killed. Those were the terms of the deal she made with the devil.

A loud rumbling engine and metal banging sounds, from the garbage truck outside, startled Melinda, causing her to momentarily shake with fear.

"It's just the garbage truck," she whispered trying to calm herself.

Sitting up and stretching, Melinda pulled herself out of bed and dressed quickly. Stepping out of her room, she walked over to the bathroom door, knocking.

"Good morning," she called out. "Are you hungry? I could make you some breakfast." Not hearing him answer, at first, she thought he hadn't heard her over the sounds of the running water. But when reaching the bottom step and seeing the front door wide open, fear struck her heart.

Racing up the steps, she found the bathroom door unlocked. Pushing the door in, a cloud of escaping steam vanished before her eyes when looking in. Robbed of her breath in finding the shower running and Sebastian gone, Melinda turned quickly. Stumbling on the hallway carpet, she went head-first tumbling down the staircase, banging her head against three spindles and landing on her back at the base of the of the stairs. Seeing stars and panting for breath, Melinda painfully rolled over, crawling on her hands and knees out to the porch. Although seeing Sebastian's jeep still parked near the barn, deep in her heart she knew he was gone.

***

Miles away, a blue garbage truck pulled into the parking lot of a truck stop.

"Thanks for the ride," Sebastian said to the driver.

"No problem, kid," the older, skinny black driver said, with a friendly smile. "Where're ya heading, anyways?"

"Boston."

"Try the trucks over there, near the gas pumps. Those are the long-haulers. You should be able to find one of them heading east," the driver suggested, pointing to his left.

"I will. Thanks, again."

Knowing it was still early in California, none the less, Sebastian pulled his cell phone out of his pocket. Finding Abdul's number, Sebastian placed a call to him. Shifting impatiently for an answer, he sighed with relief when hearing Abdul's anxious voice.

"Sebastian, are you alright? Are you safe?" Abdul asked, near frantic.

"Yeah, I'm okay. Well, I don't know," he uttered, anxiously.

"Where are you?"

"Nebraska."

"*Nebraska*!"

"Listen, you can't go home. Government agents are looking for all of you."

"I know. The agents tripped surveillance cameras when breaking in. Sebastian——."

Hearing their call disconnected, Sebastian tried re-sending, but his call went to voice mail. Seeing three truck drivers heading to their rigs, Sebastian forced his cell phone into his pocket.

"Come on, boy," he urged Silas to follow him. "Hey!" Sebastian called out. "Are any of you guys heading east?"

Chapter Six

Having spent most of the morning driving around, searching for signs of Sebastian and his dog, Melinda drove her pickup truck to a bank of gas pumps at a truck stop several miles from her farm. She'd gone to Chancellorsville first, asking anyone she saw if they'd seen a teen and his dog. After hearing no one had, she traveled down every remote, country road she thought of, still finding no traces of him. At one point, she stopped the garbage truck she thought had passed by her house hours earlier but the driver, a bald overweight man, claimed not to have seen her son or even a dog.

Intending to fill her tank, Melinda stopped when hearing a familiar voice from behind her.

"Running away?"

"I'm just filling up before I head home," Melinda answered, without looking. Her throat was dry.

"You *could*, you know, run away," Susan commented, stepping into Melinda's view. "The Nassir family has been found. We no longer require your assistance in finding them. You're free to go."

"You make it sound so easy, running away," Melinda uttered, brushing her hair away from her tear-soaked eyes.

"It is—if you want it bad enough. Go home, Melinda. Get that handsome son of yours who you fought so hard for, and just *leave*. I am a cold-hearted bitch but, I give you my word, no one will follow. The two of you can lead a normal life—somewhere far away from here."

"Yeah, that sounds pretty good."

***

Opening his eyes, Ben held still, having heard his cell door unlock. Sitting up, he placed his bare feet on the cold, concrete floor sending a chill through him. Hearing nothing other than the incessant humming from the overhead light, Ben felt his pulse racing when standing up. Wanting desperately to rush out of the cell in finding a way to escape, he took a step forward but then stopped, fearful of what might be lurking out in the dimly lit corridor.

Taking another step, when reaching the doorway, he slowly spied, out to the right, seeing pitch blackness. When looking to his left, a trail of lights leading away seemed to tell him which direction his captors wanted him to go. For a moment he thought about wandering into the blackness, yet he guessed this wasn't where they would let him to go and might have placed hidden obstacles in his path should he choose this way. Debating if he should follow the corridor to the left ended when the lights in his cell turned off. Believing his option to stay had been taken away, Ben slowly stepped out into the corridor and began walking to the left.

Taking a few steps, he noticed the lights he'd passed being extinguished, leaving him with a feeling of an animal being herded. The path ahead turned repeatedly, leading Ben to think of the corridors as part of a maze and him the lab rat searching for cheese. Passing many open doors, he lost count, wondering how many others like him had been abducted and brought here, wherever here was. Since arriving, Ben hadn't seen any other prisoners, or captors, or even the outside of his cell until now. Yet waking sick to his stomach each day, feeling as thought he'd breathed in anesthesia, Ben wondered if he had, indeed, been taken somewhere without knowing the reason.

Finally, reaching the end of the corridors, a single windowless door waited to be opened by him. Ben hesitated entering, anxious in wondering what he'd find on the other side. His captors must have known he would as the lights above him dimmed, an apparent signal for him to enter.

Pushing the door open, Ben breathed in a pungent sterile scent tainting the air. Inside the large well-lit room, he noticed how the walls and ceiling appeared to be made of rusted metal panels riveted together, reminding him of an abandoned warehouse. But when glancing at the lights reflecting off the polished grey floor, his eyes were drawn across the room to neatly lined rows of bodies. Moving nearer to them, wearing the same white jumpsuit as he was, both men and women of mostly younger age lifelessly stared up at the ceiling. Unable to stop himself, Ben knelt down to the closest one, touching a dark-haired young man's pale skin. Feeling cold to the touch, Ben quickly pulled back his hand, swallowing hard as he stood up, having never touched a dead body before.

The resounding echoes of footsteps alerted him of people approaching. Frantically looking around, he found no place to hide—except among the dead. Seeing one, remaining spot at the end of the closest row, Ben pulled a body quickly from the second row forward to that spot and then lay in the now empty space, staring blankly up at the ceiling like the others.

"Where'd he go?" a deep, husky, male voice asked.

"Damn it, he must have run out into the hallway," another man's voice responded, angrily. "I told you to lock the door once he came inside, you idiot. Come on, there's nowhere for him to run."

Hearing footsteps leaving, Ben waited a few seconds and sat up. His jaw dropped instantly when seeing five police officers standing there at attention. Yet, there was something odd about them, almost as if they weren't alive.

Approaching them, cautiously, Ben staggered back stunned in seeing how each one resembled him when wearing his police officer uniform. Taking a step to the closest one, he touched its hand, feeling no reaction from it. An impossible thought gripped him. Shedding his white jumpsuit, Ben quickly undressed one of the police officers and within a few minutes had traded places with him. Hearing footsteps approaching, he held deathly still hoping to convince the men with his deception.

Without saying a word, the larger of the two men walked over to the Ben dressed in the white jumpsuit and gripped him hard around the throat, breaking his neck.

"Put him over there with the others," the other man ordered. "Hurry up, we have to get this shipment to Boston by tomorrow. I don't want to miss the Fourth of July fireworks."

Trying to remain still, Ben's mind reeled in understanding that he'd been gone for two months and....

Drawn away from his nightmare when hearing a low growl from Sage, Ben sat up in bed, noticing how his dog's fur seemed raised on its back and its incessant staring at his bedroom door. A light, summer breeze disturbed the curtains with moonlight flooding in through the window, casting shadows on the far wall. Holding still, trying to hear the noise that had bothered Sage, but catching no unusual sounds, Ben rested his head back down on his pillow. But a moment later, he, too, heard something, causing him to sit up again.

Jumping off the bed, Sage began scratching at the door, pacing it wanting it open. Pulling his sheet off, Ben stood up, hearing the floor boards creaking under his weight. Taking a few steps, reaching for the doorknob, he stopped just short of touching it. Movement sounding out from the hallway seemed to be coming closer. Backing away, he held his breath, waiting and watching his door. The sounds stopped. Sage padded across then room, timidly, whimpering as it cowered in the corner on the opposite side of the bed.

Ben's pulse raced, seeing the doorknob turning. At first the door held still but then opened slowly, as if someone sought great care in keeping the old hinges silent. Staying hidden, Ben heard faint footsteps before seeing a shadowed movement. What he then saw sent chills down his spine. Moving further into view, his uniformed image reflected off the dresser mirror. Shuddering with fear in remembering the last time he wore his Boston police uniform, he couldn't help being awestruck by the replicate's flawless, identical appearance to him. Everything from its facial expression to the cut and style of its hair had been duplicated to perfection.

The replicate looked around the room, ignoring Sage completely. Stepping over to the open window, it leaned down, poking its head out. Thinking this might be his only chance, Ben bolted out from behind the door, causing it to slam shut while rushing up behind the replicate. With his hands extended, Ben forcefully pushed against the replicate's back, sending it falling head-first out the window. Watching the replicate flying through the air, a loud thump echoed out when its head impacted against the cobblestone patio below. Convulsing with its limbs vigorously flailing, Ben instantly flinched when the replicate suddenly exploded. Sent staggering backwards, shards of glass from the shattered windows sprayed over Ben, cutting him on his arms and bare chest.

Dazed from his head slamming against the wall, Ben tried to focus his blurred eyes through the throbbing pain radiating from his skull.

"I'm…okay…boy," he mumbled, feeling Sage licking his face. Blinking several times, a veil of smoke hung heavily in his bedroom, stinging his lungs as he breathed in the pungent stench. Noticing one of the curtains on fire, Ben unsteadily stood up, stumbling over remnants of the window frame when crossing the room. Yanking his curtain rod down, Ben thrust it and the burning curtain out the window. Coughing hard, he tried breathing in fresh air from outside, but found only heated smoke rising from below. Pulling his head back inside, Ben rushed out to the hallway, closing his bedroom door behind him in trying to keep the smoke from filtering into the rest of the house.

Stepping outside, a minute later, the coolness of the grass against his bare feet grew hot when rounding the corner of the house. Surveying the damage with a flashlight, the house siding was charred black with all the windows on this side having been shattered. Drawing the flashlight's beam to the replicate, he noticed very little left, with what debris remaining appearing unrecognizable.

Stepping back, Ben thought about what had just happened, fully understanding why the replicate came searching for him. Back during his escape, once outside the place where he'd been taken to, Ben had slipped away while the men were distracted. Eventually finding his way to Hartford, Connecticut, rather than returning to Boston, where he believed they'd eventually search for him, he headed for a hunting cabin he and his father would stay at just outside Caribou, Maine. Thinking he could protect his parents by staying away, in the end, he regretted that mistake when, months later, coming home to find his mother missing, his father dead and one of his replicates chained to a chair in the attic.

From his online research, Ben believed himself to be the only living person who'd been abducted and replaced by a synthetic replicate. Anti-government bloggers had obtained secret information about places such as the one he'd been held in, revealing the murders of all abducted citizens after the synthetic replication process had been completed.

Thinking back, his last memories before being taken were of when he was called to a domestic dispute on Boston's north side. Soon after arriving, he found the call to be a hoax, just a means for drawing him there.

Overpowered and knocked unconscious, he recalled waking up again and again in a cell, with a door and no window, until the day of his escape. But, after tonight, Ben wasn't sure if he really had escaped. He'd found one of his replicates in his attic and now he'd destroyed a second, leaving two more somewhere out there. Determined to fight for his life, Ben reasoned that either he could stay, and wait for the remaining two to come, or he could leave turning the table with *him* becoming the hunter and *them* becoming the prey.

Chapter Seven

Sitting in quiet reflection, near the back of a softly lit church sanctuary, Xavier's mother caressed the black beads of her rosary while lost in thought. Breathing in faint traces of incense, Marina glanced over to a pure, white statue of the Virgin Mary. She shifted her gaze to the subtle flickering flames of votive candles. Hearing whispered prayers offered by two nuns sitting near the altar, she silently recited a prayer of her own.

Seeing two young, Latino men enter quietly through a side door, Marina watched as they approached, finding seats in a pew behind her. She sensed them leaning forward.

"All is taken care of. The government has been led to believe your son has fled to Mexico with his family. Enough evidence suggesting they're hiding there has been planted near Mexico City. A search will be conducted and upon failure to find them, it will be abandoned. Once their file is sealed, we'll make sure it's destroyed," she heard the man on her left whisper.

"You are a good man, Ramone," Marina responded.

"Family before duty," he replied.

"As long as your son and his family stay away from San Francisco and Alaska, while also not drawing the public's attention, we can guarantee their protection," the other man added. "It would be best if they remained here in the Los Angeles area."

"Bless you, Carlos," Marina offered.

"Anything for you," Carlos said, gently touching her shoulder.

"Have either of you found out information about Sebastian?"

"Agent Susan Fletcher reported seeing him in Chancellorsville, Nebraska," Ramone whispered, leaning closer. "She has not, however, filed additional information since his initial sighting."

"Agent Fletcher has been known to be ruthless in pursuit of her leads, having received a number of suspensions and reprimands throughout her career. She's dangerous. We need to be vigilant in keeping her attention drawn away," Carlos remarked in her other ear.

"No my dear boys, we need to be more than vigilant. Our family will not live in fear," Marina murmured, with a faint sigh.

"Understood," Ramone responded.

"Sebastian must remain safe. At all costs. Quite by accident, I uncovered some information last night that I believe will lead you to him." Handing her rosary beads to Ramone, she also slipped into his palm a hand written note. "You should be able to find him with this. Leave tonight— and be careful."

Rising from their seats, both men walked away, exiting through the same door where they entered. A few minutes later, Xavier joined his mother after offering his confession to the parish priest.

"How is Abdul?" Marina asked, touching his hand, tenderly.

"He's close to falling apart—and there's nothing I can do to help," Xavier answered, exhaling deep and glancing down.

"And how are you?"

Shrugging his shoulders while studying his hands, Xavier responded, "One of my son's has gone missing—and I'm worried beyond belief for him. Sebastian *is* my son, just as Scotty is."

"And Scotty?"

"We haven't told Scotty any of what's going on."

"And you won't," Marina urged, squeezing his hand. "Scotty sees Sebastian as his brother. Were he to find out that Sebastian is in danger, he would insist on trying to help, even to the point of putting himself in danger."

"Agreed." Following a long pause, Xavier continued, "Abdul is trying his best in keeping all this hidden from Scotty but I know how it's tearing him up inside. Sebastian is all he can think about. He's all *I* can think about, too. I love both my boys so much."

"That's because you're a good father just like your father was to you."

"I miss Papa."

"So do I. The bond between Abdul and Sebastian is very strong. It reminds me of the bond you and your father shared."

"Theirs is so much stronger than you know," Xavier remarked. "I believe Abdul sees Sebastian the way he saw himself when growing up alone in Syria during the civil war. They've survived such terrible experiences yet neither can find the courage to reveal what they've gone through. Abdul has said so little about his time in Aleppo. I've never pressed him to tell me any of it. I think he just wants to forget."

"One the outside he seems so confident, so at ease. I admire him although I've never told him so."

"I wish you would. He's my rock, my constant steady anchor," Xavier whispered, smiling.

"That's how I see *you* to him," Marina offered, with a smile.

"If Sebastian doesn't come home this time—" Xavier mumbled, close to tears.

"Do not even speak it," Marina interrupted. "My *grandson* will come home."

"You've never called Sebastian that before," Xavier said, surprised.

"There are many things I haven't done that I should have." Squeezing her son's hand, "There's much I need to atone for. Now, let's go home."

***

Hearing someone approaching from behind, Abdul's eyes remained fixed on the pounding surf and the seagulls soaring above.

Upon seeing Scotty ease down on the sand next to him, Abdul held his breath.

"I just got off the phone with Sebastian," Scotty said,

"And—how is he?" Abdul asked, still keeping his sight forward while feeling both relief and fear, attempting to hide both.

"He's still sick, says he has a slight temperature, and hasn't eaten much. Gosh, it *sucks* having the flu in the summer."

Sighing, Abdul quickly understood Sebastian's lie to Scotty.

"I know. I feel bad for him." Abdul, adding to the deception. "I tried calling him last night but he must have been sleeping."

"Yeah, he said he missed your call. He'll try calling you tonight if he's feeling any better." From the corner of his eye, Abdul noticed how Scotty was staring at him, instantly knowing what was coming next. "Dad, are you alright?"

Having been told in the past in how terrible a liar he could be, Abdul knew Scotty would pursue a better answer were he to simply say 'I'm fine.' Doing something he never thought he would, Abdul deflected his answer.

"I was just thinking about the first time I saw the ocean here in California. It was just after arriving from Syria."

Hearing the hesitation in his own voice, anticipating his son's next question, Abdul knew what his response needed to be.

"What was it like in Syria? You never talk about it?" Scotty asked.

"That's because I've tried hard to forget." Exhaling deep, Abdul offered an explanation he never imagined being able to reveal, yet unable to stop himself. "Life was always hard under the Assad regime but, when warfare broke out in Aleppo that was when I was most frightened. I was a scrawny sixteen year old boy forced to become a man overnight—and I wasn't prepared for any of it."

Shifting uncomfortably, he stopped talking when Scotty reached over, resting his hand on his shoulder.

"It's okay, Dad. You don't have to tell me."

"No. I *need* to tell you. I want for you to understand. Maybe, by doing so, it will help you understand what Sebastian had gone through. Both he and I spent much time hiding, fighting for survival." Sighing, Abdul spoke further. "For me, when the bombs started falling, my family hid as best we could. My father suffered injuries, making him unable to fight. So he pushed me to join and fight with the opposition. But emotionally...I couldn't. I was too gentle, too fragile, too much a coward, too much of a disgrace."

"Being scared doesn't make you a coward or a disgrace," Scotty interrupted.

"Those were my father's words to me," Abdul revealed. "You see, I had told my mother of my *feelings* toward other men. I thought she would understand as we were so close. I begged for her to keep my secret but she told him. I can still remember the expression on his face after finding out, looking at me with disgust and hatred. I believe my confession proved the reason for us in fleeing Aleppo. Other sons went off to proudly bringing glory to their families in fighting for their fathers and I only brought shame to mine."

"I'm sorry," Scotty said, draping his arm around his dad's neck.

Following a short pause, Abdul revealed more.

"We left Aleppo during the still of the night, wandering in the darkness through the countryside. My father would find places for us to sleep and hide before the rising of the sun. For several days, all I really saw was pitch black. A week later, before reaching the Turkish border, we were halted by government soldiers. One in particular, a demon expressing an insane smirk, asked my father an unimaginable question.

'Were you to choose between taking with you only your wife or son, who would you escape with?' Without a moment's hesitation, my father chose my mother. They were allowed to leave with other refugees and I was forced to stay. Neither of my parents ever looked back. They just kept walking."

"I'm so sorry, Dad."

Feeling tears stinging his eyes, struck by how after all these years the wounds still ached, Abdul finished his confession.

"I returned to Aleppo. I didn't know where else to go. I found that our house had been bombed by the Russians. Everything was gone. So, for the next year, I hid in the ruins as best I was able scavenging for food when I could until one day when a UN aid convoy arrived in the city during a cease fire. I was befriended by a very kind, Italian doctor who ended up smuggling me out of the country. Eventually I came here to the United States, to California. My first night in my new country, I snuck away from where I was staying making my way here to the ocean. For hours I sat in the dark, listening to the sounds of the tide until first light broke, coloring the water beautiful shades of blue and pink and orange. And, at *that* moment, watching such a sublime rainbow of colors—I knew I'd found my home."

"I'm glad it was easy for you after that."

"Quite the contrary. I arrived here in America at the height of a terrible, social upheaval gripping the nation. It felt as if I'd brought with me a curse from my father. I was looked upon with suspicion and hatred, as many Muslims were during those dark years. *Eventually*, I found acceptance from most. But even to this day, there are those who still cast mistrustful glances in my direction."

"I know what you mean," Scotty confirmed.

"Someday it will be different, I hope," Abdul added.

Chapter Eight

Two days later

"You have to stay quiet, boy. I don't want anyone to know we're here." Petting the fur on Silas's head, Sebastian then climbed a set of stairs with his dog following behind. Hearing the pleasant sounds of piano music echoing off the mirrored walls, Sebastian remained hidden in the shadows, captivated in watching Lydia's awkwardly performed pirouette, yet seeing the joyful smile beaming from her. Then extending one leg away with her arms outstretched, she held this position for a moment before her arms drooped when falling out of it. The ballet instructor immediately stepped over, offering praise before demonstrating the proper technique.

Stepping behind her chair, Sebastian held still until Sidney noticed his reflection in a mirror. With her jaw dropping, she quietly stood up and walked toward Sebastian as he backed out of view just outside the dance studio. Silas lay in the corner, keeping Sebastian in his sight.

"Either I'm being haunted by a ghost or need to stop drinking," she mumbled.

Sebastian just smiled as she caressed his cheek.

"I'm looking at your father," she commented, causing his smile to slightly fade.

Needing to change the subject, Sebastian motioned toward Lydia.

"Look at her. She seems so happy."

"She loves to dance," Sidney whispered, in Sebastian's ear. Unable to look away from him, she wrapped her arm around his neck. "I'm looking at your father. My God, you look so much like him. I'm so glad you called me. You know, Lydia asks about you all the time. She'll be so excited to see you…" Her words trailed off when Sebastian stepped back, with his unspoken intention clear to her. "You don't want to see her? But, she asks about you all the time. How could you not want to see her?"

"She's better off with you, Sidney. We both know it. I know how much you love her. My dad would have wanted it this way." His regret over this must have been obvious, with Sidney reaching over, again caressing his cheek. "I *did* want to see her again but, the real reason I came to Boston—"

"Was to see your dad," Sidney interrupted, correctly guessing his reason. "Honey, I don't know how to make this easy for you."

"Sidney, I know he's dead."

"How did you find out?"

"I was able to gain access to the Nebraska program in the Daybreak chamber at my uncle's farm. Once inside, I got to talk to my dad. He told me everything he could before he disappeared from the program. I guess it was, at that moment, when he died. I just knew."

"It was." Sidney added, brushing back her tears. "I tried reviving him, but I couldn't get his heart to start again no matter what I did. He just slipped away. I'm sure he didn't suffer."

"It's okay."

"No it's *not*," Sidney quickly argued. "*Nothing* about *any* of this is *okay*. In the end, I couldn't do one thing to help."

"You're wrong," Sebastian corrected her. "I can't imagine anyone better to care for him until the end. You kept him alive long enough for me to see him one more time. And you've taken care of Lydia. As far as I'm concerned, you're her mom now." Covering her mouth, Sidney appeared overwhelmed by her emotions.

"And, did you happen to—" she uttered from behind her hands.

"See *my* mom? Yeah."

Resting her back against the wall, Sidney appeared unable to look at him. "Damn, I need a cigarette, and a drink, in the worst way." With his hand tremoring severely, Sebastian reached out, covering hers with his. Glancing down, her eyes grew large as a sigh escaped from her. "Oh, honey, it's not getting any better, is it?"

"No. That's another reason why I came here. I wanted to see if there was anything else you could do for me." Sidney seemed at a loss for words for this. "I know you injected me with that drug my dad didn't want you to."

"Yes, in a diluted form. I'm sorry. I hoped it, and the pills, would help some."

"Neither did. It's getting worse. So, I'm hoping—"

"That I'll inject you with the full strength of the drug."

"Yeah."

"Lydia will be here for another forty-five minutes," she responded, looking down again at his tremoring hand. "We live ten minutes away. I'll tell her and the instructor that I need to leave for a few minutes, to take care of a friend," Sidney said, once more caressing his cheek.

***

She checked his pulse, heartbeat, and temperature.

"Lift up your t-shirt," she instructed. "BE37 is best absorbed into the bodies system when injected through the abdomen. I'm sorry, honey. This is going to hurt." Dabbing his stomach with a cotton ball saturated with alcohol, Sidney then stuck him with a long needle, slowly injecting the drug into him. Breathing hard, grinding his teeth in feeling the burning pain, Sebastian blinked as tears streamed down his cheeks.

Then panting for breath while Sidney held him close, he finally choked out, "So, now what?"

"If this works, you should notice a lessening of symptoms in about a week to ten days. I tested a strain of Parkinson's similar to yours and, while it didn't provide a cure, the results were promising, alleviating almost all symptoms with only slight hand tremors remaining noticeable. As for side effects, the only thing I could find, and totally unexpected, is that your fertility level will vastly increase, meaning the chances of you fathering twins someday is better than fifty percent. Oh, and make sure you throw away those pills I prescribed for you. You won't need them now."

"Damn, it hurts," Sebastian mumbled. Silas seemed to notice Sebastian's pain, nudging his hand. "I'm okay boy. I'll be alright," he said, petting Silas on his head.

With the burning sensation subsiding a little, Sebastian sat up.

"Thank you," he whispered.

"You know I'd do anything for you," Sidney responded.

"Would you leave Boston if I asked you to?" Sebastian asked, thinking for a moment.

"*Why?*"

"My dad said that government agents are after anyone who had knowledge of anything to do with the replicates, people directly associated and their families. My mom tried convincing me that he was just being paranoid, a side effect of some medication you gave him."

"She lied to you."

"I know."

"Yes, your father was paranoid, but not delusional," she confirmed, sitting next to him. "His mind was always as sharp as a blade. Nothing I injected him with would have caused delusional side effects. Whatever he warned you about before he died, you need to take seriously."

"That's why I'm here. I don't want them to find you and Lydia. I want both of you to be safe. Is there anywhere else you could go, the farther away the better?"

"Well, my sister and her husband live south of Paris. She's been begging me to come for a visit. But, what about you?" Sidney answered, rubbing her brow with her hand.

"I'll be okay."

"*Will you*?"

"I hope so," Sebastian answered, trying to smile, but realizing it probably wasn't convincing. "Sidney, there's one more thing I want to ask you. Where's my dad's body?"

"The Grant Hill Cemetery, about ten blocks from here. I'll take you there," Sidney replied, sighing deeply.

"No, I'd rather walk. I need some time before I get there."

"I understand," Sidney responded, kindly smiling at him. "There's a nice hotel, Fairfield Place, a block further. I'll make a reservation there for you for tonight. By pretending Silas is a service dog, he should be able to stay in the room with you."

"Thanks."

"I'm not done," Sidney remarked. Reaching into her desk, she pulled out an envelope, handing it to him.

"What's this?"

"Rainy day money, a couple thousand dollars."

"I can't take this," Sebastian protested, trying to hand it back to her.

"Trust me. I'm richer than most people in this town, thanks to your dad. I want you to take this money, get some new clothes, and then buy plane tickets for you and Silas to go where you think you'll be safe. Promise me you will."

"I promise. Sidney—"

"Don't say another word. Otherwise, I'm not going to let you go."

***

I hate myself for what I'm about to do, but I can't find him on my own. Desperate for any information about Sebastian, Melinda drove away from her lonely farm, speeding down the road to the stop sign. Turning left, she floored the gas pedal until approaching the gas station, hoping to find Susan inside, the person she least wanted to see. But if anyone knew where Sebastian might have gone, it would be Susan. Certainly both of them remained under government surveillance. Not for a minute did Melinda believe Susan's claim that she and her son could simply walk away, never to be pursued again.

Pulling off the road, Melinda saw a red convertible spinning its wheels before leaving in a cloud of dust. Parking next to the gas pumps, waiting for the dust to settle, both her pulse and heart raced in anticipation of what would come next. As the air cleared, Melinda got out, walking a few feet before stopping to summon her courage.

Stepping into the office, a rush of hot air blown from a desktop fan unexpectedly sent a chill down her spine. A few pieces of paper blew off the desk, falling to the floor. Though not seeing Susan, Melinda did spy an electronic tablet next to the cash register. Slowly moving around to the other side, she saw a stilled image on the screen. Pressing an arrow, the recorded scene played out.

Appearing onscreen was the red convertible that had just left. Two Hispanic men, wearing white muscle shirts were leaning against the car while filling their tank. Susan must have taken a liking to their muscular sun-bronzed features, recording them without them knowing. After pumping their gas, the taller of the two walked toward the office. But the footage seemed to end there.

Hearing a sound from the single repair bay, Melinda walked over to the door, spying through the window. Her exhaled breath fogged the glass, stunned in seeing Susan hanging from a chain wrapped around her neck. Gagged with her hands bound behind her back, and her feet barely touching an overturned white bucket, what shocked Melinda most was seeing Susan alive. Her large eyes frantically shifted from one direction to the other while trying to hold still. Then locking eyes with her, Melinda couldn't understand why Susan wasn't begging for help. If anything, Susan seemed to want her to leave by how she shook her head.

Having suffered because of Susan, in the worst way, Melinda wanted to watch her die. But she needed her help to find Sebastian. With the old woman's distress growing, Melinda touched the doorknob with the intentions of helping free her. But when pushing the door in, the bucket under Susan's feet moved when struck by a broom that fell against it when the door opened. The chain around her neck tightened as she fell, strangling her. Susan's body convulsed for only a moment until her limbs lifelessly stopped moving. Noticing how her eyes looked away, Melinda glanced up to see what she might have last looked at, her heartbeat racing. A running, surveillance camera had not only recorded the last minutes of Susan's life, but had also recorded Melinda, herself, standing there watching.

Running back to her truck, Melinda could barely force the key into the ignition, then slamming on the gas pedal when speeding away. Fearing who might be watching the surveillance footage, rather than returning to her farm, Melinda kept driving staring blankly ahead with no destination in mind.

***

Hearing the afternoon breeze pass through the leaves of nearby trees, Sebastian walked passed row-after-row of headstones in search of his dad's final resting place. Shadows of clouds blocking the sun darkened the grass for a few seconds before sunlight once more bathed the cemetery grounds. Chirping birds and bouquets of flowers made this serene place seem less lonely, more like a quiet garden than anything else.

Remembering where Sidney had told him to look, Sebastian soon found his dad's small, grave marker near a large, maple tree. Glancing down at the name etched into the marble surface, swallowing hard, it took him a minute to think of what he wanted to say.

"Hey, Dad. I miss you. I'm not sure what else to say." He paused for a moment. "From what Sidney told me, I'm glad you didn't suffer and I'm glad I got to see you one more time.

Lidy is doing fine. Sidney loves her and is taking care of her so you don't have to worry. As for me, well, I'll be okay. I'm...I'm gonna go home, probably not to Alaska, and not to the lighthouse. I don't think I'll ever go back there again. Scotty and his dads are in California. As much as it scares me to go to California, that's where I'm heading tomorrow. I hope it doesn't bother you that sometimes I call both Abdul and Xavier 'Dad'. I—"

Changing the subject, Sebastian barely held his emotions in.

"I let Sidney inject me with the full strength of that drug. I know you were worried about this, but I haven't been feeling very well and I trust Sidney." Feeling a stray breeze suddenly caress his cheek, Sebastian touched his fingers to his face, reminded of how his dad's soft beard felt against his skin. Sighing with his tremoring hand falling at his side, not knowing what else to say, brushing away his tears with his other hand, Sebastian finally managed a whisper.

"I gotta go. I love you."

Part Two

Another Day

Chapter Nine

"Damn," Scotty mumbled, while furiously typing on his keyboard. It was one thing for a hacker to hack some else's data, but quite another for a hacker to find himself a victim of hacking. Conducting a diagnostic procedure on every security measure he'd installed on his computer, Scotty ran his hand over his head, completely stunned when discovering one of the program's back doors wide open.

Attempting to find the source of who breached his software, every lead he pursued found a dead end.

"Son-of-a-bitch," he mumbled, scratching his chin. Falling back in his chair, he closed his eyes, attempting to calm himself. Having no idea or evidence suggesting who had hacked his computer, Scotty agonized over his dad's finding out what he was up to. Never having wanted to lie to either of them, he understood the hurt and anger he'd face from them if they found out. And he also worried about Sebastian. What would happen to him if the information he gathered found its way into the wrong hands.

Feeling uncertain as to the scope of the security breach, Scotty glanced over at his cell phone, wondering if it too had its information corrupted by the hacker. Wanting to call Sebastian in the worst way, hoping he was safe, Scotty knew he couldn't. *What if his call would be traced?*

"Think, think, think. What can I do?" Scotty whispered, pounding his fist against his head.

***

Arriving in Boston as morning sunlight shone over the city, Ben drove his father's pickup truck to an old apartment building just north of the city's center. Stepping onto the sidewalk with his dog, Sage, in tow, the wonderful aroma of freshly, baked donuts wafting from the bakery only a half block away seemed to welcome him home. Not expecting to still have his apartment due to nearly two years of unpaid rent, he knocked on the landlord's door, expecting all his things to have been thrown out a long time ago. After knocking a second time, the door opened with a frail, old man standing there.

"Good morning, Mister Flynn. It's me, Ben Lesterman. I used to rent apartment 3A. I've been gone for a long time and was wondering if you could tell me where all my stuff ended up."

"Is this some kind of joke? You just paid your rent yesterday. Are you okay?" Mr. Flynn asked, glancing at him, oddly.

"I'm sorry, I bumped my head last night. I haven't been myself since then," Ben responded, thinking fast. Stepping back, he was confused by what was said to him.

"Do you need me to call a doctor for you?"

"No, no—I'll be alright, Ben answered. "Sorry to bother you."

Backing away from his landlord's door, Ben thought, w*hat's going on? He said I paid my rent yesterday. But that's impossible.* The answer to his question became obvious when, thinking it through, his chest tightened in fear. He cautiously climbed two flights of stairs up to his third floor apartment. Placing the key in the lock, he waited to open the door, his pulse racing, dreading what he'd find inside. Once he opened the door, when stepping in, it seemed as if he'd traveled back through time.

Everything in sight reminded him of the last morning he'd been here. An old newspaper, dated from that day, was placed on the table next to some junk mail and a stained, coffee mug. Wandering over to the kitchen sink, spider webs covered the dishes left on the counter. When opening the refrigerator door, Ben quickly closed it, covering his nose from the pungent stench of rotting food seeping out. Turning on the faucet, a burst of grey, tap water spilled for a few seconds until becoming clear.

Moving into the living room, Ben noticed a thick layer of dust covering the television screen and end tables. A thin veil of dust also shone through the beaming sunlight flooding in through a window, seeming as traces of smoke from a just extinguished fire. Crossing the room, he opened both windows, letting fresh air blow in through the partly-opened curtains.

With everything appearing untouched from when he was last home, Ben wondered why the rent had been paid with no traces of anyone living here. Glancing around again, his belief that no one had been here proved wrong when discovering something out of place. A chair, taken from the kitchen table, had been awkwardly positioned in the center of the living room, the one piece of furniture with no noticeable traces of dust covering it and a clean trail of shoeprints on the hardwood floor leading back and forth from the apartment door.

Even more concerning to Ben, though, was seeing Sage pacing near the door stopping to scratch on the wooden surface as if wanting out. But in watching him, it seemed more than a simple need to go out. Something was scaring his dog, something he hadn't found yet.

***

Having checked out of his hotel room, Sebastian and Silas wandered down a tree-lined, brick sidewalk glancing in shop windows occasionally while in search of a restaurant for some breakfast. Although he hadn't slept well during the night, the few hours of sleep he'd found made him feel better than he had in days. When waking up to sunlight, Sebastian recalled something he'd once overheard: *yesterday is the past; today's another day.*

Their relaxed pace ended abruptly as they stepped to the first intersection. Although the crosswalk sign turned green, Sebastian froze in place, shocked in seeing Ben Lesterman walking toward him. Never thinking he'd see the Lesterman's son again, he wondered how Ben would react to them meeting here. Dressed in his Boston Police Department uniform, unexpectedly he walked past both Sebastian and Silas, paying no attention to either of them. Although possible that Ben had forgotten talking to him at the Lesterman farm, what troubled Sebastian wasn't Ben's not recognizing them, but rather Silas's reaction to his former owner. Whimpering and cowering with his head hung low, Silas acted as if waiting to be punished. This reminded Sebastian of the terrible fear he'd been instilled with when expecting abuse at the boy's shelter in San Francisco.

Wondering where Ben might be heading, Sebastian turned around and decided to follow him.

"Come on, boy," he urged Silas. "I won't let him hurt you." With his dog staying close to his legs, they pressed on, keeping Ben in their sights.

Two blocks past the cemetery, Ben stopped walking when coming to a small park featuring a white gazebo surrounded by shade trees. Morning joggers crossed the open green spaces as a few, old men sat at café-style tables, two engaging in conversation while setting up a chess board. Finding a comfortable place under a large maple tree, Sebastian rested his back against its trunk as Silas lay by his side. Gently stroking his dog's soft fur, he kept his eyes fixed on Ben, who had found a seat on a bench not far from them.

While watching him, Sebastian noticed two things. Being that it was summer, Ben's pale, almost anemic complexion seemed kind of odd, reminding him of a vampire character he'd seen once in a movie. But here he sat, outside with the sun shining down on him. Maybe he had been sick, with this possibly being his first time outside in days. The other thing puzzling Sebastian was Ben's lack of reactions to anything around him; traffic noise, the barking of dogs, or even the jet flying overhead. Ben didn't seem to care about any of it while keeping his eyes fixed on the colorful blue and white façade of a Victorian-style home across the street from the park.

Abruptly rising from the bench, Ben continued staring at the house, even when its front door opened. Out on the porch, a nurse pushed someone in a wheelchair, positioning it so the person could enjoy the morning sun. Standing up, Sebastian slowly began walking across the park's wide open green space with Silas staying close to him. Approaching a wrought-iron fence at the parks edge, after glancing across the street, Sebastian took a step back, startled in recognizing Ben's mother as the person sitting in the wheelchair. He'd assumed, after being driven away from the farm in one of Dryden's cars, she had died. This left Sebastian wondering why Lexia would have taken pity on Ben's mom, letting her live out the rest of her days here in this home.

Shifting his glance toward Ben, again Sebastian felt troubled by his reaction. *Why just stand there? Why wasn't he going over there to visit her? A thought came to him that maybe Ben had been told not to, although Sebastian couldn't understand why.*

To Sebastian's surprise, Ben suddenly walked away in the same direction he'd come. With Silas following him, Sebastian set out trailing Ben across the park. Nearing two men arguing over a minor car accident, when one tried stopping Ben for help, he walked passed both men and their damaged cars, briskly, without glancing at either. They angrily shouted at him, but he just kept walking.

Turning the corner, Sebastian followed Ben for several more blocks until seeing Ben's pickup truck parked out front of an old, apartment building. Sneaking into the building after him, Sebastian looked up through the stairwell to the third floor, hearing the opening and closing of a door. With Silas climbing the steps behind him, when reaching the third floor landing, Sebastian found two doors he could have entered.

Hearing the sounds of a crying baby from the apartment on the left, not believing Ben had any kids, Sebastian focused on the door to the right. Once he'd approached what he thought might be Ben's apartment, he pressed his ear against the door's wooden surface. Hoping to hear sounds coming from the other side, the sound drawing his attention came from Silas. Pawing at the door, Silas began sniffing the floor as if capturing the scent of something.

Startled when hearing loud thumps, and breaking glass from inside the apartment, Sebastian stumbled away from the door.

"Come on Silas. Let's get out of here," he whispered, losing his nerve in being there. They rushed down the flights of stairs and left the building with Sebastian intending not to return. But, when reaching the street corner, a fiery explosion blasting out the windows of Ben's apartment sent Sebastian falling backwards onto the sidewalk. Shards of glass and large pieces of debris fell through the air, coating the street below. Dazed from hitting his head on the concrete, with Silas licking his face, the blurred vision of his eyes gained enough focus for him see a gaping hole on the third floor of the building and a cloud of smoke hanging heavy in the air.

Unsteadily standing, barely hearing the sounds of fire engines over the ringing in his ears, Sebastian covered his mouth and nose when stepping forward toward a damaged car. Feeling the blood rushing from his head, he stared at sparks shooting from the body sprawled over the car's hood, the police uniformed body of Ben Lesterman, or at least what remained of his replicate.

Chapter Ten

Feeling something hard jabbing him against his back, Sebastian heard Ben Lesterman growling in his ear.

"Keep your mouth shut and walk over to the first alley on your left. If you try to run, I swear I'll pull the trigger." Doing as told, Sebastian walked straight ahead, pausing once when seeing the dead body of a dog similar looking to Silas. Swallowing hard, he recognized it as being Ben's dog, Sage. Feeling the barrel of the gun pressing harder at his back, Sebastian quickened his pace until reaching the alley. Once out of sight from bystanders gathering around the apartment building, a blunt strike to the back of his head sent Sebastian falling to his knees. The shadowed alley and the sight of Silas nudging him blurred in his vision before fading to black.

***

Blinking his eyes open, throbbing pain radiating from the back of his head forced him to close them again. Lightheaded and nauseous, dry heaving a few times only left spit seeping from his lips with his stomach empty and aching. Bound with ropes, a sudden tremor gripping his entire body even caused the chair under him to shake. The air around him felt heavy and heated, with his t-shirt soaked with sweat.

Sensing something wet touching his hand, he knew it to be Silas's tongue licking his hand. Comforted in knowing his dog was still with him, Sebastian's fingertips lightly stroked the fur on his snout before feeling it rest it's head on his leg.

Altered in hearing footsteps sounding out somewhere behind him, Sebastian tried opening his eyes again, glancing down at Silas and the dimly lit floor. He guessed it might be Ben Lesterman there with him. He tried thinking of something to say, but with his throat painfully dry and his lips chapped and sore, he could barely mumble a sound. Wincing when swallowing deep, he opened his mouth.

"Water—please," he whispered, faintly. Silas then backed away, snarling as someone approached.

Recalling the old saying, *watch what you wish for*, his body uncontrollably shuddered when a bucket of ice-cold water was poured over his head, drenching him from head to foot. Trembling worse than he ever had before, with his head hung low he saw a pair of black shoes on the floor in front of him and then noticed another chair being set across from his. Too frightened to look up, he remained staring at the floor when hearing Ben's voice.

"Easy boy, I'm not going to hurt him…yet," Ben urged to Silas. Sitting down then across from him, Ben calmly spoke. "For months, I was locked away in a cell with a door and no windows. I think they drugged me. Every time I woke up, I felt sick to my stomach, like I'd breathed in something that caused me to sleep. I never saw anyone—until the day I escaped. Not only did I see two of the guys holding me prisoner, I also saw five men in police uniforms, looking *exactly* like me. Everyone had heard rumors of these things called synthetic replicates. But until seeing those five, I never thought that I would ever become a part of that. And there they were.

"Being that I'd been left alone with them, quick thinking, I changed clothes and places with one of them. When the men returned, one of the men broke the neck of the replicate I'd changed places with, believing it was human. In the room we were in, there were so many dead bodies. I didn't have time to count them. I was too busy thinking of how to escape."

Seeing Ben tapping his fingers against his pant legs, Sebastian breathed hard, fearing what he'd say next.

"I tried acting like the other replicates until the men were distracted by something. That was when I ran away. After breaking into a store, stealing money and clothes, I caught a ride, eventually, with a truck driver heading for Hartford, Connecticut. And, after that, I went in hiding making my way to a hunting cabin my father and I used to stay at in upstate Maine."

Seeing Ben lean forward, Sebastian's heart beat faster when hearing Ben's voice growing tense.

"Do you miss your family? I sure as hell miss mine. Every day I was away, I worried about them, hoping they were okay—and wondering if I'd ever see them again. When I finally thought it'd be safe to home, the first thing I found was the remains of a replicate at the bottom of our porch steps. Its head had been mostly blown off with its face charred, probably from the sparks."

Seeing his eyes watery with tears and hearing the distress in his voice, Sebastian listened as Ben began falling apart.

"I rushed inside the house, searching for my parents, hoping they were alright. But I never found my mother. What I *did* find was my father's decaying body in the attic...and...and...a damaged replicate which looked just like me."

Stammering to speak further, Ben's tone grew angry.

"A few months after burying my father, I couldn't take it anymore. I had to find out what happened to him. Through some research I'd done online, sites not fully blocked by the government, I found out something. Did you know that inside the heads of every replicate, there's a small camera that records images for up to a year? I had to know how my father died. So, I went up to the attic and removed the replicate's camera from its head. Then I hooked the camera up to my laptop and watched. Some of the most violent images played out on screen, murder and brutality against men, women, and even children. But that wasn't there worst of it."

"The worst images I saw came from here in the attic," Ben revealed, sniffling with his hands shaking. "I watched my mother treating that piece of garbage like it was her real son. She tried everything she could to make it real. My father did too." His anger was growing. "I saw my father's face covered with blood. I don't know how it happened but, what I do know—is that the last image shown from the camera—was of *you*."

Standing up, kicking his chair away, Ben silently paced for a moment before kneeling down in front of him. Seeing the rage so clear in his eyes, Sebastian's heart sank, knowing what Ben wanted.

"After destroying the third one of my replicates, imagine what it was like for me when rushing out of the building, and seeing you standing there, like some angel of death. Is that what you are? Are you here to reap my soul?" Ben asked, quietly, barely calm. Pausing for a moment, appearing to collect his thoughts, Ben made demands. "You are going to tell me why you were at our farm, and how my father died, and where my mother is. And you're going to tell me why months later you visited me. And you're going to tell me why I found you outside my apartment building today. Now."

Too frighten to speak, Sebastian swallowed hard, agonizing in his mind about what happened at the Lesterman farm. Thinking Ben wouldn't believe him, Sebastian blankly stared out until Ben slapped him across the face.

"Speak *now*," Ben angrily growled.

Closing his tear soaked eyes, Sebastian told his story.

"My dad and I were camping on a hill near your farm when your father and Silas found us. Your father invited us to have breakfast with them. While we were eating a storm hit. Your mother insisted we stay, but neither of us wanted to."

"Why?"

"Your mother kept calling me *Ben*," Sebastian answered, exhaling some of his fear. "She acted strange, as if I was you." Ben's eyes grew large when hearing this. "My dad and I were planning to sneak away but, then, we heard your father up in the attic. There was noise, like two people fighting. We went up there to see what happened."

"And what did you see?"

"Your dad was lying on the floor, his face covered in blood."

"Was he dead?"

"No, he was still alive, but only for a few more minutes."

Breaking down, Ben then fought to compose himself.

"Did he say anything?"

"Yeah." Sebastian revealed, looking directly at Ben. "He said he was trying to destroy the replicate because…they didn't need it anymore. They had a replacement son, *me*. He said he was going to kill my dad when he slept, and keep me as their son."

"*Liar!*" Ben lashed out, angrily, once more slapping him across the face. This time Sebastian felt blood seeping down his chin from a cut on his lip.

"*No!*" Sebastian, uttered, hearing Silas barking. Ben kicked Silas away, causing him to whimper in pain.

"My father would *never* have done such a thing." Seeing Ben pacing again, Sebastian braced himself for further abuse. Yet Ben's next question opened a fresh emotional wound. "You said your dad was there with you. Where's he at now?"

"He's dead," Sebastian answered, quietly, glancing away.

Running his hands over his face in frustration, Ben exhaled deeply.

"Why did you come back to my parent's farm? Were you planning to steal stuff or hide out there?"

"No," Sebastian uttered, shaking his head.

"Then why? Answer me."

"After everything that happened to me, I tried going home—but once there—I felt even more lost," Sebastian responded, looking directly at him. "So I left. I moved around a lot, never staying in one place too long. I guess, I went back to your parents farm because, I felt bad about what happened. And I wanted to see if you'd come back, to see if you were able to do the one thing I couldn't."

"No. I don't believe you," Ben said, shaking his own head. Then pulling a gun out from behind his back, Sebastian shuddered with fear when Ben forced the barrel just under his chin. Cocking the lever back, Ben offered no hesitation as he pulled the trigger. Nearly passing out from fright, Sebastian felt nauseous when understanding it wasn't loaded. Again Ben pressed the gun's barrel once more against his skin.

"Give me one reason why I shouldn't pull the trigger again? Maybe...there is a bullet in there," Ben asked with a rasp in his tone.

"*Because—I know where your mom is,*" Sebastian choked out, swallowing painfully.

Chapter Eleven

Riding in silence, except when directions were demanded, Sebastian stared out the front windshield of Ben's truck. Squinting and blinking a few times when oncoming headlights blinded him, his eyes regained focus of the glimmering, Boston night skyline. In knowing where they were going, Sebastian wondered what would happen when seeing Ben's mother again. *Remembering how dazed and confused she seemed the last time he saw her, he wondered if her mental state had deteriorated further. Would she recognize Ben when she saw him? And what if she didn't? How would he react?*

Handcuffed to the interior door handle, the metal seemed to be cutting off circulation to his tremoring hands. His chest started heaving, gripped by fear when Ben parked his truck across the street from the house where Ben's mother was being cared for. Striking more terror in him, as Ben got out, he glanced back into the truck.

"If you've lied to me and she's not here, the next time I pull the trigger, the bullet *will* be there."

***

Crossing the street, Ben slowly approached the house Sebastian had told him about. He read a small sign while walking up the sidewalk, Forsythe Home for the Aged, before reaching the wrap-around porch. After climbing the front steps, rather than ringing the doorbell, he wandered over to the closest window peering inside. His heart nearly stopped beating when seeing his mother sitting in a wheelchair, near the fireplace, sleeping peacefully. Anxious for her to see him, he turned to the front door, ringing the bell several times. When hearing someone approach, he stepped back, impatient in waiting for them to open the door.

"May I help you?" an older, husky black male nurse asked.

"I wanted to see Constance Lesterman. I'm her son," Ben blurted out, quickly.

"I'm sorry—but there's no one here by that name," the nurse responded.

"But—she's sitting in a wheelchair over there by the fireplace."

"You mean *Jane*? You *know* her?" the nurse asked, glancing over.

"*Jane?*" Ben confusingly uttered. "Her name's not Jane. It's Constance Lesterman."

"Do you have any proof?"

"What do you mean *do you have any proof*? What proof do you need? I'm telling you she's my mother," Ben said, his tone growing agitated.

"We need proof of identity, both for her and you. Yours *only* won't be enough. Jane was dropped off on our doorstep with no identification. That's why she was given the name, Jane, for *Jane Doe*. She's currently an elderly ward of the state. I'm sorry, but for her safety, I can't let you see her until her identity can be verified with photo identification, such as a driver's license and her real birth certificate, not a copy. Those are the rules."

Trying to barge in, Ben was stopped when the nurse pushed him back.

"You need to leave now before I knock you on your ass and call the police. Now," the nurse calmly insisted.

Staring angrily at the nurse, Ben backed away, walking down the front steps as he headed for his pickup truck. Getting in, he kept his eyes on the house, not a first noticing something he should have. After slamming his fists against the steering wheel, looking over to Sebastian, he saw that he'd fallen asleep.

"Wake up," he mumbled, coldly, when pushing on Sebastian's shoulder.

Seeing the kid slump to his side, Ben leaned over, turning Sebastian's face toward him. Gently tapping his face with the palm of his hand, Ben's jaw dropped, realizing Sebastian wasn't sleeping.

"Hey, kid, wake up!" he said, frantically, while checking to see if he was still breathing. Feeling his shallow breaths, Ben panicked, thinking he should take him to a hospital. But he knew instantly he couldn't, not wanting to reveal his being the cause of the kid passing out and everything else he'd done to him. "Damn," he growled, again pounding his fists on the steering wheel.

Believing everything was spiraling out of his control, in desperation Ben got out of his truck and again crossed the street. Peering once again through the window, he noticed his mother no longer sitting there by the fireplace. Mumbling obscenities under his breath, he approached the door, this time not ringing the bell. Testing the doorknob, finding it locked, he spied through a side window, seeing a frail, old man in pajamas aimlessly wandering by. Lightly tapping on the door, Ben got the man's attention, with him turning back and then reaching for the door knob. Once unlocked, the old man opened the door.

"Have you come to take me home?"

"Yes, I have. Go get your suitcase and then we can leave," Ben responded, thinking fast.

"I need a snack, first," the old man uttered. "I hope there's pudding, chocolate—and not butterscotch," he rambled on while walking away.

Hearing someone coming, Ben hid inside the adjacent living room just as the male nurse approached the open front door.

"Bob, did you open this again?" he asked the old man, who had now returned.

"Why, yes," the old man confirmed. "He's come to take me home."

"Who?" the nurse asked.

The old man instantly seemed distracted.

"Is there any chocolate pudding?"

"That's what I thought, sneaking pudding," the nurse remarked. "Come on, Bob. Let's get you to bed. You can have pudding tomorrow."

Seeing the nurse leading the old man away, Ben stepped out from his hiding place, turning to his left in thinking to climb the stairs to the second floor. Yet, before he could, he saw his mother step out of a room unsteadily at the far end of a dimly lit hallway. Feeling his pulse racing, he quickly approached her.

"Mother, it's me, Ben," he whispered, when moving into the light.

Concentrating on his face, his mother put her fingers to her lips while seemingly lost to thought.

"You're the police officer we brought home," she commented.

"Yes, yes, I used to be a police officer," he answered, overjoyed she remembered him being a police officer, though concerned in that she seemed to only remember the replicate.

His smile faded further when she touched his cheek.

"I read to you and sang your favorite songs. I tried feeding you but you wouldn't eat. You wouldn't even talk to me." Realizing that she was indeed talking about the replicate of himself he'd found at the house, her next words deeply stunned him. "I sent your father up to the attic after the real you came home with that strange man. We didn't need the thing up in the attic that was pretending to be you. But, the man wanted to take you away." With her eyes clearly bewildered, his mother finished. "I told your father to kill him."

Hearing so much of the kid's story confirmed by his mother's words, Ben's heart sank, with his mind reeling in knowing that he'd told him the truth. So blinded was he by his anguish over his father's death, and mother's disappearance, not for a moment did he think any of the kid's story could be true. And though Ben hated himself for what he done, if he hadn't he might never have found her.

"Mother, it's time to go," he said, quickly seeing her expression brighten.

"Is your father waiting in the truck for us?"

"No, he's at home," Ben answered, glancing away to try and control his emotions. Ben lured her by the hand. "We need to get going now. You know how grouchy he gets when breakfast isn't ready on time."

"Oh, that man," she responded. "He'll probably want pancakes and bacon."

"Yeah, I think he will."

After taking a few steps, she stopped walking, shifting her eyes as if lost. Then looking at him, she covered her mouth with her hands, as if horrified by what she saw.

"You're that thing from up in the attic. You look just like my Ben, but you're not."

"No," Ben denied, softly. "I'm your son. I'm the real Ben. I promise."

"Where are we going?" she asked, seeming more dazed than only a moment before.

"We're going home."

"Is your father waiting in the truck?"

"Yes, he is—and you know how he hates to be kept waiting."

"That's not true," she corrected him. "All your father wants to do is wait. When you didn't come home, he sat out on the porch waiting. He never came to bed that night. When we went to Boston, he just wanted to sit and wait outside your apartment building for you to come home. And then you did. Those terrible people beat you up before you could go inside. I begged him to stop them, but your father refused. He said we needed to wait. And once you did come home with that man claiming to be your father, I wanted your father to kill that man but he said we needed to wait until after dark."

"*Please stop talking*," Ben begged, almost in tears, swallowing hard. "Someone might hear us."

When finally reaching the front door, his mother stopped walking once more. Tracing her fingertips across the glass surface, she marveled at the intricate floral pattern engraved within the frosted pane.

"I had a pretty door like this. But a man came to take you away. He wouldn't leave so I grabbed your father's shotgun and blasted a hole through the door's window to scare him away. Do you think he's still out there?"

"No. I'm sure he's gone."

Quietly closing the door behind them, Ben helped his mother down the front steps and across the street to the truck. Once seated inside, another reminder from her of how diminished her memory had become surfaced when she glanced over at Sebastian.

"What's wrong with Ben? My poor boy looks like he's sick." Tendering running her hand through his hair, she then touched his cheek with the back of her hand. "He doesn't seem to have a fever."

"I—think he's just tired," Ben forced out. "Let's just let him sleep."

"What are you doing out there?" his mother asked, unexpectedly, glancing at the passenger side mirror.

Looking in his rearview mirror, Ben's eyes nearly exploded from their sockets when seeing the last police replicate of him approaching them. Quickly turning the key in the ignition while hearing, Silas's barking from the bed of the truck, Ben shifted into drive and floored the gas pedal, leaving his replicate behind.

Chapter Twelve

Blinking his eyes open, Sebastian stared out the passenger side window, seeing sporadic bursts of distant light and cars streaking passed. Sensing the constant speed of the truck, he guessed they were traveling on a highway leading away from the city. He kept his face turned away from Ben and his breaths shallow, hoping to fool Ben that he was still sleeping. But when hearing another voice softly speak, Sebastian closed his eyes, dreading what he thought might come.

"I wish Ben would wake up," Constance Lesterman whispered, while running her hand lightly through Sebastian's hair. "Do you think he needs medicine?"

"We'll take care of him when we get home," Ben answered, causing Sebastian's blood to turn cold, confirming his worst fear. In heading back to the Lesterman farm, the thought of stepping once more inside the house frightened him. He remembered everything that happened there before. In not having his dad with him he worried he wouldn't be able to handle ghost-like memories that were bound to show themselves. He opened his eyes and looked out into the passing darkness. *I can't walk into that house again*, he thought. *They'll never let me go.*

He felt a blanket being draped over him and heard Ben's mother fret.

"I'm worried about him. His body is shaking so much. Maybe this will keep him warm."

After the longest time staring out the window, Sebastian felt Ben's truck slowing down when nearing a gas station. Pulling up to a bank of gas pumps, he felt the truck stop and heard Ben turn the ignition off.

"I need to fill the tank. You two will be fine in here," Ben said, as he got out closing the door. There was something in Ben's voice that troubled Sebastian, as if Ben didn't believe his own words.

Sebastian unexpectedly felt the blanket slowly being dragged off him and then heard the keys being pulled from the ignition. He closed his eyes and what he heard next was unimaginable.

"I'm going to unlock your handcuffs but I don't want you to take them off," Ben's mom mumbled. "That machine is going to try to take you away from me. I'm not going to let that happen. When we get to the farm, I want you to run away, hide in the woods until I come find you. Do you hear me?"

"Yes, mother," Sebastian uttered, faintly, hating himself for calling her that yet thankful in her confusion she would help him. Feeling the handcuffs unlock and then the blanket being tugged over his hands, after hearing her place the key back in the ignition he waited for Ben to get back into the truck.

***

The entire time he'd pumped gas, Ben had watched every car pulling up under the canopy covering the gas pumps. Gripped with paranoia, fearing his last replicate was following them, his eyes hurt from shifting around at the other drivers, as well as searching for the security cameras. He turned his face away from them and hoped they weren't linked to surveillance that could be used to track them.

"Where are we going?" his mother asked after he got back in the truck.

Deeply exhaling, and clearly frustrated, Ben answered, "We're going home."

His mother's continuing confusion weighed heavily on him, as did the kid's health, still passed out from what he could tell. With the farm now just over an hour away, his initial plan to bring his mother home would soon be done. *What then?* Simply wanting her home with him had been his goal. No real thoughts had been given to the challenges he faced in caring for her once there. *Was she taking any medications or under a doctor's care for unknown health issues?* The more Ben thought of all this, the more he understood how unprepared he was.

Further complicating things, Ben knew he needed to make amends for everything he'd put the kid through. With each passing minute he stayed asleep, Ben worried that he'd somehow hurt him to the point of risking his life. But leaving him at a hospital proved no option, especially since his mother seemed convinced the kid was really her son. In getting rid of him now, Ben had no idea what his mother's reaction would be. Wanting to drown out all these thoughts, Ben turned on the radio, just for some noise to concentrate on.

***

After noticing the truck traveling down a dirt road, Sebastian felt it come to a stop and heard Ben turn off the ignition. Before Ben could say anything, Sebastian knew where they were.

"Mother, we're home," Ben said to her.

"Where is your father?"

"He was going hunting this morning," Sebastian heard Ben lie.

"I wasn't talking to you," his mother said, coldly. "I was talking to Ben but he still won't wake up."

Clearly noticing tension and emotions in Ben's voice, Sebastian heard him say, "I'll wake him up after I help you into the house."

Moments later, after hearing them get out of the truck, Sebastian turned his head, seeing them at the front door and then step inside. Having slipped off the handcuffs as soon as they were out, when seeing the door close behind them, as quietly as he could Sebastian opened his door.

"Silas, here boy," Sebastian whispered, standing unsteadily. Jumping down from the bed of the truck, Silas padded over to him, licking his tremoring hand. "We need to get out of here. Come on, boy." Lightheaded for a moment, Sebastian staggered away through thick bushes at the edge of the yard. Trudging on, within minutes, he couldn't see the house anymore.

Once he'd reached the crest of the hill above the Lesterman farm, to the east Sebastian saw traces of reddish first light coloring the horizon. But when looking to the west, the sky appeared darker than it should. The delicate rumbling of rolling thunder sounding out told why.

***

Ben followed his mother into the kitchen and watched as she traced her fingertips over the granite countertop and touched the faucet above the white farmhouse sink. Keeping quiet, she moved over to the antique white stove, wrapping her fingers around the handle of a black tea kettle. She took a step back and opened the oven door, peering down in and then looking away in confusion.

"I was baking cookies for Ben, but the pan is missing."

"You burned them, so I had to throw the pan away," Ben snapped, impatiently, growing further unnerved by her continued thoughts that the kid out in the truck was her son.

"Yes, I did burn them. I can smell the smoke," she responded, seemingly lost in thought. In truth, light traces of smoke still hung in the air from when Ben's replicate had exploded outside, damaging some of the house. Carrying the tea kettle over to sink, she filled it with water and then placed it on one of the front burners.

"Here, let me light that for you," Ben offered, striking a match to ignite the gas flame. While doing this for her, she found a mixing bowl and flour from the pantry. Stepping back, he watched as she began preparing breakfast, appearing as she had so many other mornings, even humming while she worked.

Happy in seeing her content and distracted with cooking, Ben intended to quietly leave her there, wanting to step out to his truck to check on the kid. But as he turned toward the door, her words startled him.

"You won't find Ben. I unlocked his handcuffs and told him to run away and hide until you left."

Rushing out to the porch, he felt his heart in his throat when seeing the passenger door of his truck open and the kid missing.

"Damn it," he growled, running over to find his handcuffs on the seat and no traces of which direction the kid and Silas had gone. Torn with thoughts of wanting to find them, but also knowing he couldn't leave his mother alone, bursts of lightning and a clap of thunder offered him no respite from his dilemma.

Thinking the kid might turn him in if he made it to the local police, Ben knew he had to go after him. He fetched a combination lock from a tool box in the bed of his truck. He sprinted up the porch steps to the front door, securing it with the lock in hoping to safely keep his mother inside. Then running through the yard, he headed up the hill, in the direction of the nearest town.

Ben moved fast and, within a few minutes, he'd reached the tree line at the top of the hill. Glancing back, the western sky looked to be growing darker. And then before his eyes, bolts of lightning splintered out across the sky, resembling an instantly vanishing spider web. The ensuing clap of thunder reverberated through the air, causing the ground under his feet to shake.

Catching his breath, the flashing of headlights from the nearby road wearily drew his attention. Seldom ever did vehicles other than the mail truck drive anywhere near the farm. But with the appearance of two cars, one pulling off to the side of the road farther back than the other, fear struck him deep that they'd been followed. Sneaking over to some tall brush, when spying through, he exhaled his anxiety, seeing two young men changing a flat tire on the closest car. And not seeing the other car, he hoped it was innocently just passing through.

Pressing on through the trees, low wind-bent branches slashed across Ben's face, one cutting him across his cheek. With forceful gusts pushing against his back, he continued on until reaching a tall-grassed clearing. Silas's deep growl threateningly halted Ben in his steps, seeing the kid panting for breath while standing unstable by the strong winds howling through the trees. Ben reached out his hand and begged forgiveness.

"I'm sorry I hurt you. I'm sorry for everything I did to you. I know there's nothing I could say to change what happened. But *please*—let me help you." Reminded of the coming storm by a brilliant burst of lightning, Ben urged, "Please come back to the house with me. I can't leave you out here in the storm. There's food and a soft bed back at the house. Let me tend to your injuries and then you can leave. I'm not going to hold you against your will. I promise, not again, never again. I was wrong. Please, come back. Please." Taking a step toward Sebastian, Silas moved between them, growling once more. "Easy, boy. I'm not going to hurt either of you."

Struck on the back of his head by a large branch wrenched from a tree by the wind, Ben fell face-forward down to the ground. Dazed with pain throbbing from his skull, when rising to his knees, through blurred eyes Ben saw that the kid and Silas were gone.

Chapter Thirteen

Distracted by the chimes echoing from a grandfather clock, Constance looked up from her mixing bowl. Confused by her surroundings, she wandered away from the kitchen, passing through a darkly lit hallway to the living room where she turned on a table lamp. A picture on the mantle, above a river-stone fireplace, caught her attention. Walking over to it, she removed it from its place and held it in her hands, her fingers gliding over the frame's glass. Smiling at her and Thomas's wedding photograph, a thought occurred to her that she hadn't seen her husband. She wondered where he was and returned the picture to its spot on the mantle before turning to begin searching for him.

Flashes of lightning flooding in through the living room windows revealed her image back to her from a wall-mounted mirror. Tracing her fingers down her cheek, she cringed at how terrible she appeared. Her hair was a mess and she lacked any sort of makeup on.

Not wanting to be seen looking like this by her husband, Constance climbed the steps to the second floor. She found her bedroom, turned on a light, and sat before the mirror of her vanity table. Applying a thick layer of powder to the apples of her cheeks and nose, the last thing she did was to add lipstick. Pursing her lips, the wide red ring she drew around her mouth seemed more fitting for a clown, but she failed to notice this. After smearing mascara around her eyes, Constance fussed a bit with her hair before placing a short-brimmed hat on her head.

Standing up and shedding her pink nightgown, she reached into the back of her closet and pulled out her faded, white wedding dress. Grinning with her selection, within minutes she managed to mostly pull on her dress, though stretching the fabric to its limits over her sagging, petite frame and unable to reach the back zipper. Checking her appearance in a floor length mirror, she sighed contently, now ready to see her husband.

When she stepped into the dark hallway from her bedroom, a loud explosion of thunder caused the attic door to rattle open. Noticing lightning flashing down from the attic, a vague memory recalling the need to go up there forced her other thoughts aside. Nearly tripping over the hem of her dress, she reached the door, pulling it open as another burst of lightning lit the dark stairwell. Slowly climbing each step, her hand flowed across old wallpaper until finding a light switch. Flicking the lever up, the attic darkness vanished in dim light.

Stacked off to the side were dust-covered boxes of seasonal decorations and old clothes. Also stored among the clutter were an old television and a trunk. But what held her eyes firm was a man's lifeless body lying near the small window. Kneeling down next to it, Constance covered his hand with hers and then gripped his fingers. Scooting closer, she turned his face toward hers, seeing his one remaining eye blankly staring at her and the damaged mechanisms exposed from behind his face. She pulled his head onto her lap and tenderly stroked his cheek.

"Mother's here, my precious child. Your father and I won't let them hurt you anymore," she whispered.

Hearing loud knocking from downstairs, Constance pulled the body even closer.

"The bad man has come to take you away," she uttered, in a hushed voice. "I won't let him take you. I promise." Leaning down, she kissed his cheek, staining his skin with red lipstick marks. Easing him off her lap, she rose and left, leaving the light on for him.

She returned to her bedroom and pulled open her top dresser drawer. Feeling around under some clothes, she smiled when finding the something hidden she was searching for. Tightly grasping the handle of a small gun, she lowered it to her side when descending the staircase while still hearing pounding on the front door.

**

Pelted across his face by the driving rain, Ben staggered through a field of storm-blown, tall grass while trying to find his way home. Having lost sight of the kid and Silas, he'd given up hope of finding them, abandoning his search until at least after the storm passed. Concerned for his mother, Ben pressed on, expecting to see lights from their house once reaching the crest of the next hill. However, when he emerged through the tree line, air rushed from his lungs, startled in seeing headlights coming from a car parked next to his truck. Again fearing that his last replicate had found them, he bolted across the open field, stumbling twice when tripping over large fallen branches hidden within the grassy slope. *You son-of-a-bitch, stay away from my mother.*

When reaching the edge of the yard, he skidded to a halt, watching helplessly as a dark sedan pulled away. He knew he didn't have the strength to run after it. Lightheaded, he staggered toward the porch but fell forward into a puddle next to his truck. Pulling himself up, he walked unsteadily the rest of the way, climbing the steps to find the front door still locked. Turning the dial with the right combination, once the lock fell to the floor, Ben forced the door open. The ricochet of a bullet hitting the door's metal frame sent him diving for cover under the kitchen table.

"Ben, Ben—is that you?" he heard his mother ask. "The bad man has come back. He wants to take you away." Overwhelmed in fearing both his replicate and his mother with her gun, Ben held still, trying to think of what to do. He thought of showing himself to his mother, reasoning with her to lower her gun. But he knew that she still didn't recognize him as being her son. The risk seemed too great at this point. *Think, dumbass,* he scolded himself. *How do I get that gun away from her?*

Seeing the fruit cellar door to his right, after silently counting to three Ben scurried on his hands and knees across the kitchen floor over to the door, drawing more gunfire from his mother. Once inside, he quietly closed the door behind him, climbing down the dark steps in looking for a place to hide until coming up with a plan.

He watched the outside, cellar door open and banging in the wind. Crouching down by the furnace, he worried he wasn't alone down here. Reaching around in the dark, he found what he thought might be an old jar. Testing to see if his replicate might be hiding nearby, Ben tossed the jar, with it shattering when hitting the concrete floor. He waited and felt relieved when nothing reacted to the sound. Easing out from his hiding place, he cautiously approached the outside door.

Again pelted by driving rain stinging his face, once outside, he searched around the side of the house for a trellis. Although the wood was wet and time worn, he hoped it would hold his weight as he climbed up to the second floor. But after breaking two pieces midway up, he soon doubted it would. Looking up, seeing his closed bedroom window less than an arm's reach away, he noticed the window on the attic dormer partly open. He knew from there he could climb into the house without breaking a window. He decided to risk this and climbed faster, passing by the second floor. With the trellis teetering under his weight, Ben had barely crawled in through the open window before it collapsed.

Tripping and falling over something in the dim light, a flash of lightning shone the familiar replicate lying next to him on the floor. Ben eyes were immediately drawn to the smeared lipstick on its cheek, certain it wasn't there the last time he'd seen it. Now anxious in thinking his mother had come up here, Ben believed her state of mind had worsened. Clearly suffering with dementia while holding a gun made her just as dangerous as the replicate he believed might also be lurking inside the house. Burying his face in his hands, Ben felt helpless, having no idea what to do next.

Resounding gunshots heard from the first floor jarred him. Although he loved his mother, Ben now realized the mistake he'd made in finding his way back into the house. With the trellis having collapsed, he knew climbing out window to escape was no longer an option. Also, knowing it would be too far to jump from the window to the ground, the only way out was down the steps and out the front door.

Glancing over at the replicate, the memory of his last escape flashed in his mind, leading him to a desperate thought. *He'd done it before. Could he do it again?* He stood up and quickly shed his drench clothes, replacing them with the replicates police uniform. Then dressing the replicate in his shirt and jeans, he dragged it over to the window, positioning his head in the shadows to hide the gaping hole in its skull. He cleaned its cheek of his mother's lipstick and smeared what he'd collected on his fingers over his own cheek, hoping to complete the deception.

Ben heard the creaking of the attic steps. He tried lying in the same place where the replicate was, doing his best to hold still while lifelessly staring out. Just as his breathing went shallow, his mother appeared from the dark stairwell, gun in hand. With her expression seemingly despondent, at first she pointed the gun's barrel at his head, cocking the trigger. Unable to hold still, Ben swallowed hard, closing his eyes as he waited to die. But after a terrible moment passed, he opened them again, seeing her still standing over him. While her hand shook, her eyes lost sight of him, shifting back and forth. Apparently noticing the replicate near the window, she wandered away, pointing the gun in its direction.

"You hurt my boy," she mumbled, and fired the pistol.

Flinching with the loud sound of the gun's discharge, Ben nearly passed out when his mother dropped the gun. Landing next to his head, the barrel threateningly pressed against his skin, just above his eye. He lay paralyzed in fear, staring at it and expecting it to fire on its own. It didn't.

Reaching down, his mother picked up her gun, studying it as if seeing it for the first time.

"I wonder what this is doing here?" she mumbled. "How strange. I wonder if it's loaded." Then pointing the gun at herself, she pulled the trigger.

Chapter Fourteen

Crouching down low, in some tall grass under the end of a trestle train bridge, Sebastian stroked Silas's soaked fur, hearing his soft whimpering complaints.

"I'm sorry, boy. This is the best place I could find for us to hide. I just can't go back to that house." Partially shielded from the heavy rain, both of them shuddered with chills from being drenched. The sounds of the raging flow of the river water below the bridge competed with the rolling thunder. With the storm maintaining its intensity, Sebastian looked out at the morning sky, appearing more as if moments after nightfall.

Sebastian remembered crossing this bridge with his dad and knew of a small town only a mile down the rails. The quickest way to get there meant crossing the bridge. Otherwise it would take twice as long by traveling on the nearest road. Fearing Ben Lesterman might be driving in search of him, he knew that walking the train tracks would be safer than finding the nearest road, if he could find the courage to do so.

Nervously running his hand over his wet jeans, Sebastian felt something in his pocket. He reached in and pulled out the old pocket watch his dad had given him for good luck. Although tarnished and not having kept time for about a year now, he studied the stilled hands while running his fingertips over the crystal. Hoping it might hold some more luck, Sebastian looked at Silas, seeing his dark gentle eyes staring at him.

"I'm cold and tired. I don't think the storm's going to let up soon. What do you say, boy? Do you want to go for a walk?" With his ears perking up and his tail wagging, Silas clearly understood what was asked.

Crawling out from under the bridge, the driving rain instantly stung Sebastian. Silas vigorously shook but held his head low while staying close. They wandered up to the rails leading across the bridge. The distance to the other side was lit by several, rapid bursts of lightning. Appearing narrow with the length possibly that of a football field, he knew crossing this bridge would be treacherous because of wide gaps between the railroad planks. Taking a deep breath, Sebastian and Silas started out, slowly taking step after step as wind-driven sheets of rain seemed to shake the trestles.

Losing his balance, Sebastian teetered for a moment before steadying. Erupting echoes of thunder and violent outbursts of lightning remained their companions as they continued on.

"I don't know about you, but I think it's going to quit soon," Sebastian called out, trying to lie to keep himself going. What he really wanted to do was turn back and wait out the storm. Getting away from Ben and his mother, though, won the argument over staying.

When reaching the center of the bridge, a thought occurred to him, something he should have considered before they started out. Sebastian wondered when the next train was due to pass through. Thinking back to crossing with his dad, they'd wondered the same thing and were fortunate in not seeing any trains that day. Trying to force this dilemma from his mind, Sebastian continued on with Silas keeping close.

***

Hearing his mother's gun fail to fire, Ben released a shallow exhale of relief. Clearly startled by flashes of lightning, she took a step back, staring down at the replicate she'd shot. Ben watched her every move and saw the confusion clouding her expression. This broke his heart. Before bringing her back here to the farm, he'd wanted to find her, hoping she was still alive. After taking her away from the nursing home in Boston, caring for her was to become his priority. But seeing his mother like this, completely robbed of rational thoughts, he knew the mother he once loved was gone. He guessed the drugs developed within the last decade to halt and reverse the effects of dementia in patients would be far beyond helping her.

Hearing the attic door open, footsteps sounding out from the creaking steps soon revealed that which Ben dreaded most to see. He tried holding deathly still and forced a blank expression across his face when seeing his last replicate emerge from the shadowed stairwell.

His mother turned toward it, not acting as if it was an intruder. A smile brightened her face as she reached for his hand.

"Ben, dearest, you made it home. We were so worried about you. Your father has been looking forward to this hunting trip for weeks now. I'll go find him for you," she said, starting to head down the staircase to the second floor. But she stopped.

"What am I doing here? Do I know this place?" she uttered, glancing around looking thoroughly confused.

"Go downstairs, Mother. I'll be down in a minute," the replicate responded, calmly. Nodding her head in understanding, she slowly left, leaving Ben wondering if he'd ever see her again.

Hearing the fakeness of the replicates tone, sounding nothing like his own voice, Ben's heart sank further hurt by his mother failing to notice that it wasn't her son's voice she heard. But he understood this to be yet another part of her dementia.

Approaching silently, the replicate looked down at Ben, studying him with its penetrating stare. Holding his breath, Ben hoped his rapid pulse and heartbeat wouldn't betray him. A loud clap of thunder then seemed to become his ally, drawing the replicate's attention over to the open window.

Watching it step away, Ben noticed how its stare had fallen on the other replicate. Praying for the impossible, that he'd fooled both his mother, and this last replicate, he knew he couldn't hold still much longer. Maybe it would believe that nothing else remained here to kill, mission accomplished. Yet, as this thought passed through his mind, Ben remembered something he'd read on line, leaked classified information referencing elite, replicate assassins. Knowing what stood there near him, Ben clenched his eyes closed, gripped by fear.

***

The sparks from a bolt of lightning, striking one of the trestles, sent an electrical charge through the metal rails. Feeling it coursing through his body and hearing Silas's whimpering, Sebastian knew they had to get off the bridge for fear of being electrocuted. Looking forward, for a moment the tracks ahead were clear. But after taking another step, Sebastian stopped when a flash of lightning revealed what appeared to be a man standing at the end of the bridge. As he turned around, a much brighter burst of lightning shone two men standing side-by-side at the far end behind them. Scared in thinking they might be replicates, his heart sank in his chest. *This is it, I guess*, he thought to himself.

Knowing he lacked the strength to fight off two men, Sebastian stepped forward with Silas staying close. He shuddered with fear, his heart pounding in his chest, as he wondered if he should jump into the river below. He knew he was too exhausted to fight the rapid current and believed he and Silas might be swept away, possibly drowning before they could swim to shore.

Adding to his sense of hopelessness, the resounding pitch of a distant train whistle frightened him. With the bridge already vibrating from the storm, there was be no way to tell which direction the train would come. Drawing closer to the man ahead of him, Sebastian wondered if he could overpower him enough to get away.

Stepping near him, with the train whistle seeming louder, a burst of lighting revealed the man's face. Black and mature, possibly fifty-ish, the blankness of his expression led Sebastian to believe he might be a replicate as well. Holding no weapon in his hand, his long trench coat and fedora gave him the appearance of a gangster from a classic, black and white, Hollywood film.

A sudden ground-shaking explosion knocked Sebastian down, causing him to wince in pain from his back landing against one the rails. Glancing behind him, he saw a ball of fire and billowing smoke rising over the woods, blending in with the dark clouds overhead. He recognized the direction it appeared from and guessed that something terrible had happened at the Lesterman farm. But he wasn't sad in seeing this, feeling only relief instead.

Nudged by Silas, Sebastian stood up shakily, massaging his throbbing back as he stepped forward. Too disheartened and weak to try to fight these men off, over the sounds of the storm Sebastian called out to the man ahead of him.

"I just want to go home! Please!" Not speaking a word, the man took a step forward, reaching his hand out.

Looking beyond the man, the piercing whistle of an oncoming freight train sounded out before seeing the headlight from the engine rounding the bend. Fear-stricken, staggering forward, Sebastian grew lightheaded as his rain-blurred vision clouded to shadows.

"I've got you," he heard a man's voice say while feeling a hand grab hold of his arm as he stumbled away from the tracks. A rush of wind from the speeding train, robbed him of his breath as he fell to his knees. Feeling

Silas licking his cheek, he knew they were safe, at least for the moment.

"Who—are—you?" Sebastian asked, through trembling words.

"Consider me a friend," the man replied. "Allow me to help you up. My car is not far from here. We need to get out of the rain."

Sometime later, Sebastian opened his eyes after having fallen asleep. Seeing a blanket draped across him, slight movement on his lap made him look down, finding Silas's head resting in his lap there in the back seat of the man's car. Softly stroking the fur on his dog's head, Sebastian stared forward, watching the headlights of oncoming traffic through rapidly swishing windshield wipers. The blue and red lights lit across the dashboard reminded him of the interior of the Dryden company car Abdul had driven when they were escaping San Francisco. This time his dad wasn't there protecting and comforting him, but at least Silas was. Although still frightened by what had happened, and not knowing where they were going, his eyes felt too heavy to stay open. Futilely blinking to stay awake, the sounds of the rain and droning of the wipers soon lulled him to back to sleep.

Chapter Fifteen

"I still can't believe what I'm about to do," Scotty remarked, while walking down the Santa Monica Pier next to his grandmother. "Never in a million years would I have imagined anything like this."

"Have you told anyone?" Marina asked, quietly, leaving him stunned she would even think such a thing.

Fully understanding that one doesn't just go around shouting, *hey, everyone, I'm gonna be a spy*, he quickly answered.

"No."

"As it should be," she commented, with a grin. "After all, that is the primary rule, never to tell anyone what you are." She motioned with her head. "Just look around you. Any of these people could be one, the jogger over there or the ice cream vendor or the fisherman."

"I guess a person could get paranoid, wondering the true nature of total strangers," Scotty commented.

"That seems to lend itself to the age old question, *does anyone really know another person?*" his grandmother remarked.

"How am I going to pull this off?" Scotty mumbled, doubting himself.

"That's the easy part," Marina revealed. "You're going to live in the dormitory at UCLA and attend your advanced technology classes. What other students won't realize is that specialized projects and coursework designated solely for you will *actually* be government sanctioned assignments. The degree you're pursuing warrants independent study. Not being allowed to share your theories and ideas with the other students in the program is clearly stated in the degree summary. So, go and enjoy your college experience like thousands of other student will. And, when people ask what you're working on, either keep your answers vague or bore them death with overwhelming technical details. I'd chose vague answers if I were you."

"So, when did you become one?" Scott asked, hesitantly, after sharing a smile with her.

"Just after coming here to the United States," his grandmother replied, appearing to think her answer over. "A few weeks after your grandfather was found murdered in Colombia, I fled to Los Angeles with you father and his sisters. Being that your grandfather was well connected with the government in Bogotá, I was familiar with many of the powerful and elite in my country. Roughly a month after arriving, when approached by an American DEA agent, an offer was presented to me, one I couldn't refuse. From that moment on, I had become—." Marina stopped herself before saying the word.

Unable to keep himself from smiling, Scotty shook his head.

"Do you know how crazy all this sounds?"

"Yes, I do," she answered, wrapping her arm with his.

"So where would you go?"

"Back to Colombia, Mexico City, Santiago, Buenos Aires, anywhere I was needed," Marina answered, quietly, thinking for a moment. "After two years, I left the DEA when an offer was made for me to join a branch of the Secret Service, the branch you're joining."

"And my dad and aunts never knew?"

"And still don't," she confirmed.

"Wouldn't they wonder why you'd leave all the time?"

"The cover I created for myself proved believable. Marina Carteras, an international romance writer venturing off to literary conferences around the world. I'd only be gone a week at a time. They never suspected."

"Just for the sake of asking, you don't really write those books, *do you*?"

"Not one word. I have a talented ghost writer who completes this task for me."

"Have you two ever met?"

"No. The manuscripts are sent directly to the publisher. I receive a copy after the final edits and formatting have been completed."

"Have you ever read any of them?"

"*Every one.* Just because I didn't write them doesn't mean I'm not a fan."

Arriving at the farthest end of the pier, Scotty looked out to the sea gulls soaring through the clear blue sky. Breathing in the ocean's salty fragrance, he looked at her.

"I still don't understand this. Why would the government offer this kind of job to an eighteen year old kid like me?"

Marina wrapped her arm around his waist.

"You're no *ordinary* eighteen year old kid. Your aptitude for computer hacking has astounded technology experts at the highest level, leaving them all speechless with your creative abilities in breaking through the most sophisticated security systems."

"But I don't do anything extraordinary," Scotty argued.

"That's *precisely* what sets you apart from all others, my dear grandson. Security experts across the world are engaging daily in cyber warfare, using the most advanced technology available. But what they fail to understand are the most *simplistic* paths to breach their safeguards. The most brilliant minds in the world fail to fathom that they've overthought *everything*."

Thinking back, Scotty remembered what Lee Dryden had said to him the first time they met. *Why did I bother hiring the brightest minds in computer protection—*

with not one of them being able to stop a teenage boy from hacking into our most secured data?

A remark his grandmother made pulled him from this memory.

"Just wait until they find out how talented you are with surveillance." His forced frown must not have convinced her as she smiled at him. "Remember my dear, *this* is an area of my expertise."

"What gave me away?" Scotty asked, reluctantly.

"We'll discuss this later in private. Trust me when I say this, you nearly *did* get away with it."

"Do you think he'll be angry with me?" His emotions were rising.

Kissing him on his cheek and squeezing his hand, Marina replied, "I know he'll forgive you."

"How do you know? You've never met him."

Leaning her head against his shoulder, Marina responded, "I just know he will."

"What about my dad's? When they find out how much I've lied to them, I'm not sure they'll forgive me, especially Abdul."

Smiling, Marina offered her thoughts.

"Speaking as a parent, we know at some point our children will lie to us. Some lies are innocent with their intentions—and then there are some lies that seem unforgivable. But, believe me when I say this, nothing you have done is unforgivable. They love you. They will understand."

***

Sebastian opened his eyes and watched as a light breeze disturbed the curtains of an open window near his bed. Hearing soft snoring, he leaned his head up, smiling when seeing Silas asleep at the foot of the bed. But there was one more sound capturing his attention. He glanced at his palm. His jaw dropped when finding the pocket watch his dad had given him. The quiet ticking of the seconds hand revealed the watch having somehow been repaired. Everything appeared polished and in working condition, much better than when he'd taken it from his dad.

A black man, wearing a well-tailored suit, startled him when entering the room without knocking. Reacting before he could, Silas's low growl greeted the man.

"My apologies for awakening you," he offered, seeing Sebastian alert.

"I wasn't asleep," Sebastian responded. He instantly recognized the man as being the one who pulled him off the train tracks.

"What's your name?" he asked, curious to know who the man was.

"Maurice," he responded, while taking hold of Sebastian's wrist in checking his pulse.

Again, Silas growled.

"Easy boy. He's not hurting me."

"Your canine companion has hardly left your side in the three days we've been here. I believe we've developed a bond. I've only been bitten by him twice."

"Sorry about that."

"You shouldn't be," Maurice corrected him. "The devotion your dog has displayed is a direct reflection of the care you've shown him." Reaching his hand out, Silas licked his fingers as his tale excitedly wagged.

"Where are we?" Sebastian asked, resting his head back down on the pillow.

"Two miles north of Bar Harbor, Maine. I brought you here to this safe house to care for your injuries. You suffered with exhaustion, dehydration, and concussion-like symptoms. I believe you will be feeling much better in a day or two."

"And—why were you there at the bridge that night?"

"I was sent there for you," Maurice responded, matter-of-factly.

"Who sent you?"

"I was instructed not to reveal that to you. However, when you are well enough to travel, this information will be provided for you."

"Who were the other men at the bridge?"

"They were not with me and I have yet to find out their identities. Having no clear knowledge of how, or when, they arrived, I am certain they will remain a mystery unless they expose to you their motives for being there."

"Could you at least tell if they were replicates?"

"They were indeed human."

Curiously studying Maurice's face, Sebastian suddenly was struck with fear.

"Are you a replicate?"

"Yes, sir, I am a synthetic replicate. Do I frighten you?"

"Yeah, a little, maybe a lot."

"Why?" Maurice inquired.

"The only replicates I've ever been around were trying to kill me."

"I find that your fear of replicates has been enhanced by your unfortunate circumstances when in direct contact with them. Synthetic replicates are, in fact, inherently docile. It is human programming that makes them dangerous. Therefore, I believe your fear should be more directed to their human creators who have turned them into weapons."

"Are there still a lot of replicates out there?"

"Until recently, my conducted research concluded that I was the last of the synthetic replicates. However, additional information has to come to light, altering this conclusion."

"What additional information?"

"Once more, the American government has lied to its citizens in concealing a classified, synthetic, replicate program having deemed it too valuable to abandon. One thousand additional replicates, spread out across the country, are existing in a government enacted *Replicate Hibernation Initiative.* They have blended into their communities, appearing as ordinary citizens until called upon when their true objectives are assigned to each."

"Are they dangerous?"

"That is unclear, sir. No additional information has been made available."

"So—none of this is over," Sebastian commented, deeply exhaling. Maurice's blank expression seemed to reveal his not knowing a response for this. As Maurice turned to leave, Sebastian asked one more question. "When I was on the bridge, I saw an explosion. Do you know what happened?"

"A house exploded," Maurice confirmed. "The local authorities believe a natural gas leak to be the cause."

"Was anyone hurt?" Sebastian asked, holding his breath in waiting for the answer.

"Two bodies were removed from the rubble. Due to significant burns, neither could be identified. It is believed they were the homeowners."

Once alone, Sebastian got out of bed and walked into the adjacent bathroom. Turning on the shower, he waited until the water seemed warm enough before stepping in. With his mind reeling in knowing more replicates were out there, waiting for human programmers to awaken them to unleash their true purpose, he slouched down in the shower stall. Pulling his knees up to his chest, his body shuddered with crippling fear, thinking their pursuit of him would never end.

Later, wiping the shower's steam off the bathroom mirror, Sebastian gazed at his tired reflection. He pushed aside any thoughts of crawling back into bed. In truth, what he really wanted was to run and hide the way he had before. But, even when doing that, he couldn't outrun his fear.

Running one hand through his longish wet hair, what struck him most when tracing his other hand across the lightly bearded shadow on his face was how much he looked like his dad. He recalled people having told him this before, causing him to miss his dad even more. Thinking now about him, Sebastian remembered his confidence, even when knowing how hard he'd try hiding his fear.

"I wish I was like you," he whispered to his reflection, pretending it was his dad staring back.

Chapter Sixteen

Finding the latest model MP3 player with headphones and new clothes and a new backpack on the bed, Sebastian listened to classic rock music while sifting through the clothes. After getting dressed in jeans and a button-down white shirt, with Silas padding along behind him, he left the bedroom. He found Maurice sitting in front of the television. Sebastian smirked.

"So that's where you get your information, cable news networks."

"I find it useful in keeping up with current events," Maurice responded. "Although my internal information database is linked to numerous political, social, and environmental sources, I find them lacking with the human element, being that of correspondents and network anchors. I continue to be perplexed, though, by sarcasm."

Wandering over to a wall of floor-to-ceiling, clear glass windows, Sebastian looked out to waves crashing against the jagged shore below the beach house, now realizing how it was perched on a cliff. Seemingly peaceful seagulls soared through the partly cloudy sky, their flights at times suspended in midair as if caught in strong updrafts.

"Excuse me, sir. I have a video message from someone you know waiting to be played for you. I will pull it up on screen when you are ready."

"Go ahead, play it for me," Sebastian said, sitting down on the sofa with Silas resting under his feet. Stroking his dog's soft fur with his toes, he heard Silas's content exhale as a familiar face appeared on the television screen.

"Hey, there," Scotty seemed nervous in greeting him. "I thought it would be easy, just talking into the camera—but it's not. "I…" he paused, awkwardly glancing away. "I…want you to see something. Here goes."

Feeling his heart in his throat, Sebastian's jaw dropped as images of him appeared on screen. Although understanding how extensive modern day surveillance captured footage from almost everywhere, the thought never really occurred to him that he'd been watched in such a way. Screen shot after screen shot, taken that year following his escape from One Legacy Place, shone across the television screen. Sebastian quietly sat there, stunned in seeing himself working odd jobs at construction sites in Tucson and Santa Fe. And there appeared footage of him running carnival rides at county fairs in rural Kansas and Missouri. Finishing out the images were moments showing him wandering here and there, seeming just as lost as he felt at this moment.

"Please don't be angry with me," Scotty revealed, returning to view onscreen. I was worried about you. I'm *always* worried about you. So, I placed a tracking chip in the pocket watch your dad gave you. By hacking into global satellite networks, I was able to follow you. When I found out where you were, I kept you in sight by accessing local surveillance databases, keeping an eye on you as much as I could. What I want you to understand—is that I could never let anything happen to you. If even for a moment I thought you'd be in danger, I would have done everything I could to help. I hope you get what I'm trying to say. You're not just *like* a brother to me, you *are* my brother." Seeing Scotty's emotions overwhelming him, Sebastian felt his own eyes water as Scotty blurted out, "I love you...and...I need you to come home. I need to be able to worry about you in person," he added, attempting to smile. "*Please*, no more running. Come home, not to Alaska—but here to southern California. It's not scary here like it was in San Francisco. I promise."

"Please don't be angry with me for sending a replicate to find you," Scotty added, appearing to compose himself. "Maurice is extraordinary. When I found out that the government was going to have him terminated, I intervened and saved him. He's been working for me ever since. He won't hurt you, maybe bore you to death with details, but I think you'll survive. Trust him. He'll help you find your way home."

With Scotty's face disappearing from the television screen, Sebastian sat there, staring away for the longest time. *California, the place he dreaded most, was where Scotty wanted him to go. Safe, what did that mean?* Sebastian remembered so many times thinking he'd found a safe place, only to be spooked away by demons haunting his mind or by people acting suspicious, causing him to be afraid.

"Should I confirm airline reservations to Los Angeles for both you and Silas?" Maurice asked, disrupting Sebastian's struggling thoughts.

He paused before answering.

"Yeah," Sebastian responded.

"Should you like, I could list Silas as an emotional service dog. That was he could fly with you in the jet's main cabin rather than in animal storage."

"Thanks. That would be great." But as Maurice appeared to be linking his replicate brain to secure flight reservations, Sebastian interrupted him. "How far are we from Welsh Cove?"

"Approximately six miles north, sir."

"I'd like to stop at my dad's lighthouse before we leave Maine."

"As you wish, sir."

***

The kettle's high-pitched whistle barely registered in her mind as Melinda stood next to the vintage, white stove. Distracted by thoughts of her son and the sacrifice she made to save him, only when a small bird collided with the window above the kitchen sink, did she snap out of her trance. Removing the kettle from the burner, Melinda poured the boiling hot water into a mug and dipped in a tea bag. She looked out the window. The growing overcast, grey skies seemed to match the lifelessness she felt inside herself. Clinging to this one place, a symbol of a life she once led, her eyes searched around the lonely lighthouse cottage as if expecting to see a ghost. In truth, that's what she wanted. If only Lee's ghost would appear before her, confirming her death. But then what? This place wasn't heaven but, instead, a private hell. Thinking this, it felt right to linger in such a dark place. For the terrible things she'd done, she deserved nothing less.

Too restless to sit in front of the fireplace and watch the burning log turn to ash, Melinda took her hot tea with her as she climbed the lighthouse's circular staircase. When reaching the top, she stepped out to the observation deck. Struck instantly by a robust easterly gale, her mug slipped from her grasp, falling and shattering on the jagged rocks below. She backed away from the railing and brushed strands of her wind-blown hair away from her face while watching the ocean swell turn to white foam when washing ashore.

Glancing down to the beach, Melinda's heart nearly exploded through her chest in seeing Lee dodging the crashing waves rolling over his feet. Hands in pockets with his unbuttoned shirt blowing in the wind like a cape, she found herself entranced in watching him, remembering him best when he wandered alone along the shore. But in a split seconds time, her precious memory vanished when seeing a dog run up to him. Overwhelmed with emotions, she knew that moment she'd mistaken her son for Lee.

Stepping back, hoping to remain out of sight, Melinda reached in through the open door, fetching a pair of binoculars hanging from a hook just inside. She spied through the lenses. A grin crept across her face, seeing

Sebastian's peaceful smile while playing in the surf with his dog. This is how she always imagined him being.

She rushed down the lighthouse staircase. When finally reaching the cottage front door, a thought corrupted the joy she felt in seeing Sebastian again. Believing herself being the cause for his leaving, a selfless notion grew in her mind. *I've hurt him worse than anyone deserves to be. I can't do that again. I need to make this right. I have to.* Thinking he would never see her without remembering what she'd done, and desperately wanting him to be happy, Melinda decided to make one more sacrifice. Casting away her desire to be with her son, she reached out, locking the cottage door. Then taking a step back into the shadows, she waited in silence.

Sebastian walked slowly up to the door. Holding her breath, she willed herself the courage to let him go. Noticing his apprehension as he stopped walking, her heart broke seeing how his hands trembled and how he shifted his weight nervously. He then appeared to summon his courage. Sebastian stepped forward until he was lost from her sight through the window. Staring at the locked doorknob, she watched it turn in vain. She heard a soft thump against the door and imagined him resting his head against the surface. And her heart sank deeper when hearing his spoken words through the open window.

"Come on, boy. No one's here. It's time to go."

Shuddering in fear of never seeing him again, struggling to catch her breath, Melinda wandered over to the door. She touched the wooden surface as if a sacred treasure once certain her son was gone. She then rushed back through the cottage and quickly climbed the lighthouse stairs to the observation deck. Winded and crying, she saw Sebastian and his dog walking away, down the shore until out of sight. With them they, unknowingly, took her heart.

***

Sebastian moved away from other passengers waiting to board the flight to Boston. He studied his ticket for there and the other for the connecting flight to Los Angeles. A tremor suddenly gripped his hand. Unable to continue reading the information, he glanced out a large floor-to ceiling window and watched a jet taxying to a runway. He then looked over at an exit sign over a metal door. Taking a step toward it, he stopped and swallowed hard, unsure of what he should do.

"Which way is home, boy? I wish I knew," he mumbled, looking down at Silas who stood by him.

Seeing a happy, young Chinese couple walking hand-in-hand and reminded of an old Journey song, "Send Her My Love," which he'd just listened to through his headphones, a thought crossed his mind. From his pocket he pulled out a cell phone Maurice had given him. Scrolling through cell phone numbers, he never thought her number would be there and was surprised when he came across it. *I shouldn't call her. I'm sure she doesn't want to hear from me,* he thought. But after a moment thinking further against his judgement of this, he called her anyway.

"Hello," he heard Nikki answer.

"Hi. It's—Sebastian."

"Wow, hi." Following a short pause, she continued, "I wasn't sure I would ever hear from you again. How are you?"

"I'm...okay, I...guess."

"Liar."

Sebastian nervously smiled. "Yeah."

"Where are you?"

"I'm in an airport in Portland, Maine."

"Where are you heading?"

"I...have tickets for Boston and then on to Los Angeles," he answered, while looking again at the exit sign.

"Are you going to get on the airplane?"

"I don't know," he answered, swallowing hard and feeling his heart in his throat.

"Sebastian, go home. Go to LA. You'll be safe there."

"What if…it's not…safe?"

"Then I'll come and rescue you again." Hearing her say this caused him to smile a little and hesitate to speak.

"Sebastian, are you still there?"

Before he could answer he heard an airport attendant over the intercom.

"First call for Flight 735 to Boston."

"Sebastian?"

"Yeah, I'm still here. Hey listen, I gotta go."

"Okay."

"Nikki!"

"Yeah."

"I was, I mean—I…well, I was wondering…if you still had a thing…for soft grey eyes?"

Hearing the heaviness of her voice lighten he smiled when she answered.

"Yeah, I always will."

"Maybe—I could call you sometime, if that's—okay."

"Call me tomorrow night, and every other night after. Goodbye, Sebastian."

"Bye," he uttered, feeling the butterflies in his stomach surging.

Silas nudged his tremoring hand. Glancing down, Sebastian petted his head and then looked at both the line of boarding passengers and again at the exit sign.

***

The next day

Hearing the soothing drone of the surf crashing in upon the shore, competing with the sounds of Xavier's restful snoring, Abdul sat up in bed. Having tossed and turned all night, his mind rampant with worrying over both Scotty and Sebastian, he crawled out of bed and left their room. When stepping out onto the terrace, he unexpectedly found his mother-in-law staring out at the ocean. Marina noticed him.

"Good morning," Abdul greeted her. "I wasn't expecting anyone else to be awake?"

"I have to be at LAX in a few hours," Marina replied, after sipping coffee. "I was invited at the last minute to a romance writer's conference in Lima, Peru. I should be gone for about a week." Seeing her odd glance toward him, Abdul knew what she would ask. "So, why are you up so early?"

"I guess I just can't sleep," Abdul responded, shrugging his shoulders.

"That is because you are good father. Both of your sons are gone and you're overwhelmed in worrying about them," Marina remarked, expressing a knowing smile.

Abdul swallowed hard.

"I know one is safe—but it's killing me inside not knowing about the other."

Placing her hand over his, Marina corrected herself.

"I was wrong. You're not a good father. You're one of the best."

Abdul grinned.

"Compliments from you, what is the world coming to?"

"I will deny them to my grave," Marina answered. "I have my reputation as a bitch to uphold."

Leaning over, Abdul kissed her on her cheek.

"I will deny this to my grave. I also have a reputation to uphold."

Marina moved closer to him.

"I know how to ease your suffering. Take a walk along the beach. The sounds of the pounding surf, the fragrance of the ocean, the calls of the sea gulls, combined—they have a way of washing away all worldly troubles. Go on, dive into the waves and allow your soul to be cleansed."

Following her advice, Abdul changed into his board shorts and wandered down to the sandy beach. But, before touching the water, he saw a young man and a dog sitting there on the sand. Slowly walking up to them, Abdul first recognized Silas, resting peacefully next to Sebastian. Overwhelmed in finding them both here, Abdul quietly sat down next to Sebastian, who remained staring out to the ocean. Unsure of what to say to him, Sebastian must have guessed his struggle, rescuing him with his words.

"I'm scared."

"Of what?"

"Everything," Sebastian answered, breathlessly.

"You don't have to be," Abdul replied, placing his hand on Sebastian's bare shoulder, feeling his body trembling with fear. Scooting closer to him, Abdul wrapped his arm around him with Sebastian resting his head against Abdul's shoulder. "Let me be scared for you—so you can be at peace. You're safe. I promise."

"I'm not sure I'll ever feel that way again."

"It will take time. I hope someday you'll feel different. Until then, I'm not going anywhere. You have my word."

"Okay." After the passing of several silent minutes, Sebastian whispered, "I want to tell you everything."

"And I want to hear every word," Abdul responded. "But not today. Tomorrow; tomorrow is another day." Kissing him on his forehead, Abdul held Sebastian's tremoring body close as they watch the faint colors of first light explode with brilliance at the exact moment of daybreak.

The End

About Jeffery Martin Botzenhart

Sebastian's journey has come to an end. Thank you for following his story. If you have read my other books then you are familiar with how boring I am. Now, my friends, confession I guess, is good for the soul. So here it is. As a teen, I was bullied for six years in school and never once said a word to anyone in hopes of stopping it. From that point on I have suffered with social anxiety. Yes, I'm now married and have three sons. I have a job and a quiet social life. But if you were to ask me what I most would desire, it would be a secluded beach, a good book, and the sounds of waves crashing on the shore. To me, that is heaven.

Social Media

Facebook:
https://www.facebook.com/jefferymartinbotzenhartwritingjourney/

If you enjoyed this story, check out these other Solstice Publishing books by Jeffery Martin Botzenhart:

Daybreak – Nightfall Book One

Amidst a world of cyber surveillance and advancing technology of 2035 San Francisco, Sebastian, a teen runaway, innocently access a sophisticated virtual reality program. The breach of this data proves the catalyst in unraveling corporate and government sanctioned deception of the most unimaginable type. And along with his computer hacker friend, Scotty, both are thrust into a dangerous conspiracy, linking them to a source exposing the truth.

https://bookgoodies.com/a/B073SB9BXG

After Dark – Nightfall Book Two

With Sebastian's health deteriorating, his dad decides to risk them both crossing into Canada in efforts to meet with a physician friend in Montreal who might be able to help. Yet before even reaching the border they encounter new threats against them. Their escape is further complicated when after reaching Lee's friend they are separated. This leads Sebastian to a perilous journey across the Canadian frontier, finding both a new friend and discovering a far more dangerous robotic conspiracy than anyone could have imagined.

https://bookgoodies.com/a/B0778SL11P

Dead of Night – Nightfall Book Three

Sebastian's hopes of having a new life in Alaska quickly fade. Suffering in being the constant target for teasing from his high school classmates and understanding the dangers his dad attempts to shield them from, a sudden tragedy destroys any chances of this. He returns to San Francisco with the belief he can resume his previous life there as a runaway surviving on the streets. But as the old saying warns, *you can't go home.* The dangers he faces here have multiplied, leading him to wonder if he can ever escape from the relentless hauntings of his past.

https://bookgoodies.com/a/B078SCFX77

Harvest Fever

A bullied and abused teen boy's plans for escape from a small remote town in Appalachia are hindered by a space alien invasion. Finding everyone in town missing, the aliens begin hunting him. And after being captured, he discovers the unimaginable truth of what's really going on.

https://bookgoodies.com/a//B074JZV44F